Deep in the metal
It was a harsh, alie
in it, but the pain
were clear enoug
through the trees, growing louder, drawing
nearer. More voices rose on every side, the deafening chorus cutting at Silence like a knife, and
he shrank back against the tree trunk even as he
raised his gun in a futile gesture of defiance. Guns
weren't going to stop what was coming for him.
Shadows moved in the swirling mists, encircling
him, and Silence caught brief glimpses of clawed
hands and snarling mouths, large graceful forms
and flat-planed gargoyle faces.

He took aim and fired his disrupter. The crackling energy beam smashed through the nearest
face and shattered the tree trunk behind it. There
was a loud rending sound as the tree toppled
slowly over and crashed to the forest floor.
Metallic shrapnel pattered down for some time,
but there was nothing to show he'd hurt or even
scared his enemy. He hadn't really expected anything else. His enemies were already dead; ten
years dead. They just wouldn't admit it and lie
down.

Ghostworld

SIMON R. GREEN

VGSF

First published in Great Britain 1993
by Victor Gollancz

First VGSF edition published 1993
by Victor Gollancz
A Cassell imprint
Villiers House, 41/47 Strand, London WC2N 5JE

A catalogue record for this book
is available from the British Library

ISBN 0 575 05388 7

Printed in Great Britain by
Cox & Wyman Ltd, Reading, Berks

Contents

Inside Base Thirteen, nothing moves. Doors remain closed, elevators are still, and shadows lie undisturbed. One by one the flickering lights gutter and go out, and a growing gloom stalks the empty steel corridors. The few computers remaining on line mutter querulously to each other in the growing dark, until finally they fall silent in the night.

In the silence, in the dark, something stirs.

CHAPTER ONE

Something in the Storm

The *Darkwind*'s pinnace fell away from the mother ship, a gleaming silver needle against the endless night. It hung for a moment above the Rim World called Unseeli, and then its nose dropped, the engines roared silently, and the pinnace slipped into Unseeli's churning atmosphere like a knife into a belly. The engines burned bright, powering the slender ship through the violent storms by sheer brute force. Lightning flared round the pinnace's hull, and winds gusted viciously from every side, but nothing swayed the ship from its course. It punched through the roiling clouds with arrogant ease, dropping like a stone towards the metallic forest below.

Unseeli had no oceans and no mountains, only an endless arid plain covered by a brightly shining forest stretching from pole to pole. A forest whose colossal metal trees knew nothing of leaf or bud, autumn or spring. They rose unbending from the grey earth in their millions, cold and unfeeling, like so many gleaming metal nails. Towering almost to the edge of the planet's atmosphere in places, the huge trees stood firm and unyielding against the turbulent storms. Winds whipped viciously around leafless branches that radiated out from smooth featureless trunks in needle-sharp spikes. Violet and azure, gold and silver and brass, the trees reached up into the thunder and lightning to welcome the falling pinnace.

Captain John Silence sat slumped in his command chair, watching the sensor display panels before him. They changed from moment to moment with bewildering speed, far too fast for him to follow. Which was why the ship's Artificial Intelligence was piloting them down, and Silence had nothing to do but strain his eyes at the displays. The thick storm clouds hid the metal trees from sight, but the AI picked them up on the pinnace's sensors and changed speed and direction accordingly, making decisions and evaluations in split-second bursts. The AI could think faster and react more quickly than Silence ever could, even when he was mentally linked to the onboard computers, so there was never any question as to which one of them would get to pilot the pinnace down. But the AI was programmed to be considerate of people's feelings, so it might let him actually land the pinnace, if it didn't seem too difficult.

Silence's scowl deepened, and he accessed the pinnace's sensors through his comm implant. The bulkhead walls before him were suddenly transparent as the sensors displayed a real-time simulation of what was happening outside the ship. Dark, swollen storm clouds rushed towards and around the pinnace at heart-stopping speed, and lightning struck viciously at the ship. Silence winced inwardly, but kept his face calm so as not to upset his passengers. The storm could rage and spit all it liked, nothing could harm the ship as long as its force Screen was up. Gleaming metal trees appeared and disappeared in the blink of an eye as the pinnace surged this way and that, threading a path through the metallic forest to the landing pads by Base Thirteen. The storm clouds were too thick and too dark for Silence to make out the forest itself, but his imagination pictured it as an endless, vicious pincushion; solid metal spikes waiting for him like the sharpened stakes at the bottom of a pit dug to trap animals.

The image disturbed him, and he cut off the display and swung round in his chair to see how his passengers were doing. A good Captain never neglected his crew. Supposedly, loyalty was programmed into them these days, but it never hurt to be careful.

The ship's young esper, Diana Vertue, was looking distinctly green about the gills from being tossed around by the pinnace's sudden changes in direction. Investigator Frost sat beside her, cool and composed as always, her face almost bored. The two marines, Stasiak and Ripper, sat behind the two women, passing a gunmetal flask back and forth between them. Silence's mouth tautened. If he was lucky it was just alcohol, and not some new battle drug they'd cooked up in the medlabs. Officially he was supposed to encourage such initiative, but Silence didn't believe in chemical courage. He preferred the real thing, whenever possible. Chemicals wore off.

'We'll be touching down soon,' he said evenly. 'There shouldn't be any immediate danger, but keep your eyes and ears open anyway. Due to the urgent nature of the situation, we're going in pretty much blind on this one. The mission's simple enough. Base Thirteen isn't answering any calls. Our job is to find out why.'

'Question, Captain?'

'Yes, esper Vertue?'

'According to the computers, Unseeli is a dead world. Nothing's lived here since all indigenous species were wiped out after the Ashrai rebellion, ten years ago.'

'That's right,' said Silence, as the esper paused.

'But if that's the case, Captain; if there's nothing on this planet that can harm the Base, why all the panic? It could just be a case of cabin fever. It's not exactly unknown, out here on the edge of the Empire.'

'A good point, esper. But four days ago, Base Thirteen declared a Red Alert emergency, raised a force Screen, and cut off all communication with the Empire. The Empire doesn't like being cut off. So, we're going in to find out what's happened. Don't frown, esper; it'll give you wrinkles.'

'I was just wondering, Captain; well, what is the Investigator doing here?'

'Yeah,' said Investigator Frost. 'I've been wondering that too.'

Silence took his time about answering, openly studying the two women. They made an interesting contrast. Diana Vertue was short, slender and golden-haired, and reminded Silence very much of her mother, Elaine. The young esper had only just turned nineteen, and had that arrogant innocence that only youth can produce and maintain. She'd lose it soon enough, trying to maintain law and order and sanity out on the edge of the Empire, among the newly developed Rim Worlds. There was little civilisation to be found on the new frontier, and even less law, never mind justice.

Investigator Frost was only a few years older than the esper, but the difference between them was that of the hunter and its prey. Frost was tall and lithely muscular, and even sitting still and at rest, she looked dangerous. Dark eyes burned coldly in a pale, impassive face, framed by short-cropped black hair. The jolting descent didn't seem to be bothering her at all, but then, it wouldn't. Investigators were trained to withstand much worse than this. Which was at least partly why they made such efficient killers.

The Captain realised he'd let the silence drag on longer than he'd intended. He leaned forward in his chair, frowning as though he'd just been marshalling his thoughts, knowing even as he did that he wasn't fooling the Investigator one bit.

'You're here, Investigator, because we don't know what we're going to find when we get down there. There's always the possibility that Unseeli has been visited by some new alien species. This is the Rim, after all, where starships have been known to disappear into the long night, never to be seen again. And aliens are your speciality, are they not?'

'Yeah,' said Frost, smiling slightly. 'That's one way of putting it.'

'On the other hand,' said Silence, 'Unseeli is a mining planet, and the metals extracted here are of vital importance to the Empire. Any number of factions might have an interest in disturbing production. Which is why I'm overseeing this mission myself.'

'If it's that important, why are there only five of us?' said marine Stasiak. 'Why not go in mob-handed with a full Security team, surround the Base, and then charge in and hammer anything that moves?'

'Because Base Thirteen controls all the mining equipment on Unseeli,' said Silence steadily. 'Systems are already running at barely thirty per cent efficiency. We don't want to risk damaging the Base and making things even worse. And, as the esper pointed out, there's always the possibility this is just some new form of cabin fever, and all the Base personnel need is a nice little chat with the *Darkwind*'s psych department. We're here to find out what's going on and report it in, not run a crash-and-burn mission on the only people who can tell us what's happened.'

'Understood, Captain,' said the other marine, Ripper. 'We'll run this one nice and easy, by the numbers. No problem.'

Silence nodded curtly, and studied the two marines unobtrusively. Lewis Stasiak was average height, average weight, only early twenties but already looking hard-used and running to seed. His hair was a little too long, his uniform a little too sloppy, and his face had a kind of slackness to it. Silence recognised the danger signs; Stasiak had gone too long without any real action or challenge, and grown soft and careless. Which was at least partly why Silence had chosen him for the exploratory team. If something went wrong, Stasiak wasn't going to be any great loss. It was always useful to have someone expendable on hand, to send into dangerous situations before taking a look for yourself. Still, he'd do well to keep an eye on the man. Marines who got sloppy tended not to last long under pressure, and when they finally did snap they had a nasty habit of taking down anyone who happened to be with them at the time.

Alec Ripper, on the other hand, was everything that Stasiak wasn't. Ripper was a career marine, and looked it. Twenty-nine years old, fourteen years in the Service, big as a brick outhouse and twice as mean. Sharp and tidy from his close-cropped head to his shiny boots. Four medals, and three

commendations for courage in the field. Could have
been an officer, if he'd only had the right Family
connections. As it was, according to records he'd
been a non-comm twice, busted both times for daring
to suggest a superior officer might just possibly be
wrong. That wasn't wise, in the Service. Especially in
front of witnesses. Also according to records, Ripper
was a good soldier and a better fighter, with a positive
gift for survival. If anyone was going to come back
alive from this mission, it was him.

If anyone was.

They didn't know about Unseeli. Silence knew.
He'd been here before, ten years ago, when the
Ashrai came sweeping out of the forest in endless
waves, slaughtering every man and woman in their
path. He remembered the awful things they'd done,
and the even worse thing he'd done to stop them.
The Ashrai were dead now. Extinct. Along with every
other living thing on the planet.

The pinnace lurched suddenly to one side, the roar
of the engines seeming to falter for a moment before
regaining normal rhythm. Silence spun round in his
chair and glared at the displays before him. Warning
lights were flaring red everywhere, but there was no
sign of any actual damage yet. He accessed the sensors
again, and the ship seemed to go transparent before
and around him. Dark storm clouds boiled around
the pinnace, streaming away to either side with
breathtaking speed. The ship lurched again, and

Silence's stomach quivered in sympathy as the pinnace changed course and speed with reckless indifference to its passengers' sensibilities. Glowing metal trees appeared and disappeared around them, come and gone in the blink of an eye, but Silence could tell the pinnace wasn't just trying to avoid them. There was something else out there in the storm. Something that had waited a long time for revenge, and didn't give a damn that it had been dead for ten long years.

Ghostworld.

'Marines; man the guns,' said Silence harshly. 'Investigator; access the sensors and tell me what you see. Esper; I want a full psionic scan, as far as you can project. I need to know what's out there.'

The marines' faces went blank as they accessed the pinnace's fire controls through their comm implants, their eyes filled with what the gunsights showed them. The Investigator's cold face hardly changed at all as she looked quickly around her at bulkheads that were suddenly transparent. The esper looked at Silence uncertainly.

'What exactly am I scanning for, Captain?'

'Something, anything; for whatever's out there.'

'But . . . there's nothing there, Captain. It's just a storm.'

'No,' said Silence. 'It's not just the storm. Run a scan, esper. That's an order.'

'Aye, sir.' The esper's face became fixed and unseeing, and her face was suddenly blank and untenanted as her mind leapt up and out beyond the pinnace.

The storm boiled around her, but could not touch her. Metal trees burned in her mind like brilliant searchlights plunging up through the clouds, guttering here and there as automated mining machinery tore through a tree's roots. Apart from the trees there was no life anywhere in range of her esp, and yet it seemed to her that there was something at the edges of her mind, sensed only as swift flashes of movement and an occasional feeling of being watched. Diana forced her esp to its limits, pushing at the range of her scan, but was unable to get a clear sight of whatever it was. If there was anything at all . . .

Stasiak grinned nastily, feeling the pinnace's guns swivelling back and forth, responsive to his thoughts. Four disrupter cannon, state of the art and fully charged, scattered the length of the pinnace and ready to kick arse at his command, or merest whim. But there was only the storm and the wind and the endless bloody trees. According to the sensors, there was nothing out there worth firing at. He found a secure line and patched into Ripper's comm implant.

'Hey, Rip, you see anything?'

'No. But that doesn't mean it's not out there.'

'Yeah, sure. You ask me, the Captain's got ants in his pants over nothing. This world's dead, Rip; everyone knows that.'

'Maybe. There's nothing on the sensors. But I still

keep getting the feeling that we're not alone up here. Stand ready, Lou. I don't like the feel of this at all. And if it does all hit the fan, don't waste your shots; place them carefully. Remember, these cannon take four minutes to recharge between each shot. A lot can happen in four minutes.'

'Yeah, right.' Stasiak stirred unhappily in his seat, trying to look every way at once. Now that Ripper mentioned it, he could feel it too. Something waiting, watching, hiding just out of range of his sensors. His mind caressed the fire controls, feeling them respond like hounds straining at the leash. The pinnace's AI was programmed against activating the guns itself except in the direst emergencies, to keep it from getting ideas above its station, but it sensed something was wrong about the storm too, and in its own way was just as eager for action as he was.

Investigator Frost looked across at Captain Silence. 'Sensors all report negative. There are no life signs registering anywhere within their range.'

'I didn't think there would be,' said Silence, staring unblinkingly out at the storm. 'Odin; how long till we touch down?'

'Twelve minutes and forty seconds, Captain,' said the AI promptly. 'Assuming nothing interferes with my flight plan.'

'Get us down fast, Odin,' said Silence. 'Marines; stand ready. Something's coming.'

And then the pinnace lurched suddenly to one

side, the slender craft thrown violently off course as though some giant hand had reached out from nowhere and swatted it. The ship bucked and heaved as the AI fought to keep it from crashing into the tightly packed trees. Dark shapes loomed up out of the boiling storm clouds, huge and threatening.

'Odin; raise the force Screen,' said Silence, his voice calm and steady, though his hands were closed into white-knuckled fists. 'Marines; pick your targets carefully. Investigator; what do you see?'

'Still nothing, Captain. Sensors are adamant there's nothing out there.'

'Same here,' said Stasiak urgently. 'There's nothing to aim at!'

The pinnace shuddered as something impossibly huge pounded against the force Screen, again and again. Silence watched tensely as his displays showed mounting pressure building up against the Screen from all sides at once. Glowing trees whipped past faster than ever as the AI sent the pinnace racing through the metallic forest, heading for the landing field. But despite the pinnace's increasing speed, the dark presences stayed with them, battering at the force Screen with vicious determination.

Silence scowled, and licked his dry lips. 'Marines; lay down a field of fire on both sides. Random selection of targets. Do it now!'

The marines' replies were lost in the thunder of the disrupter cannon, and blinding energy leapt out from the pinnace, striking through the Screen and shattering the metal trees. Great metallic shards flew like shrapnel. And still the unliving presences pressed close around the Screen, the pressure rising impossibly moment by moment.

'Our guns are useless now until the energy crystals recharge,' said the Investigator quietly. 'And the force Screen isn't going to last long enough for us to reach the landing field. It's taking more and more of the ship's power just to maintain the Screen, and we don't have that much power to spare. Not if we ever want to get off this planet again. What's out there, Captain? Why don't they show up on our sensors?'

Silence looked at her. 'Because they're dead, Investigator. Because they're dead. Odin; time to touch down?'

'Ten minutes, twenty-two seconds, Captain.'

'When I give you the word, drop the Screen and channel the extra power to the engines. Do whatever you have to, Odin, but get us down. If we survive the landing, we can always recharge the ship's batteries at Base Thirteen. Marines; stand ready to fire again, on my order.'

'But there's nothing out there!' said Stasiak. 'There's nothing to aim at!'

'Keep the noise down, Lou,' said Ripper calmly. 'Ours not to reason why, remember? Just do what the nice officer says. At least he seems to have some idea of what we're up against.'

Stasiak sniffed mutinously. 'They're not paying me enough for this.'

Silence glared out at the storm, and looked back at the Investigator. 'Anything on the sensors?'

'Negative, Captain. No life signs of any description. As far as the instruments are concerned, we're alone up here.' The Investigator looked at him with cold, hard eyes. 'You were expecting this, weren't you, Captain? That's why you came down with us. You know what's out there.'

'Yes,' said Silence. 'I know.'

'Guns are powering up, sir,' said Ripper. 'Ready to fire again soon. Just find us a target.'

'Stand by, marines. Esper; talk to me. What do you see out there? Esper!'

They were huge and awful and they filled her mind, blazing like the sun. Too strange to measure, too vast to comprehend, they gathered in the storm like ancient vengeful gods, striking at the pinnace with thunder and lightning. Diana Vertue struggled to maintain her own sense of identity in all that rage and fury, but her human mind was a small and insignificant thing in the midst of such intense, bitter hatred. She retreated back behind the safety of her mental shields, fighting to keep out the inhuman thoughts that roared and howled in the storm outside the pinnace. One by one her defensive barriers slammed down, and suddenly she was back in the pinnace again, and Captain Silence was shouting at her.

'It's alive,' she said dully, her mind feeling slow and awkward now that it was working only on the human level again. 'The storm's alive, and it hates us.'

'Have you made contact with it?' said Silence. 'Could you communicate with it?'

'Communicate with what?' said the Investigator sharply. 'If there was anything alive out there, the sensors would show it!'

'They're too big,' said Diana Vertue. 'Huge. Vast. I've never felt such hate.'

'Try,' said Silence. 'This is why I brought you with us; to talk to . . . what's out there.'

'No,' said Diana, tears burning in her eyes. 'Please. Don't make me . . . the hate hurts so much . . .'

'Do it! That's an order!'

And Diana threw her mind up and out again, into the storm. Espers always obeyed orders. Their training saw to that. Those who couldn't or wouldn't learn didn't live to reach an adult's estate. The storm raged. Immense, dark thoughts were all around her, and she knew she only survived because she was too small for them to notice. She also knew that in a slow, creeping way, they were beginning to realise that someone was watching them.

Silence watched the young esper's face contort from the horror of what her blind eyes were seeing, and wouldn't let himself look away. If she died or lost her mind, it would be his responsibility. He'd known the risks when he'd insisted on her as part of his team. A thin line of saliva ran slowly from the corner of her mouth, and she began to moan softly. Silence still wouldn't look away.

'Marines; lay down a covering fire, random selection, as before. Odin; lower the Screen. Hang on to your seats, everyone. The ride's about to get a bit bumpy.'

There was a deafening roar, slamming against the mind as much as the ears, as the dark shapes pressed forward, no longer held back by the force Screen. The disrupter cannon blazed through the storm, and could not touch them. The pinnace shuddered and lurched from side to side, tossed like a leaf in a hurricane. Metallic trees a dozen feet thick leapt out of the clouds and slammed against the pinnace sides, but the ship's hull had been designed to withstand disrupter cannon and low-level atomics, and they held easily against the battering. The thunder of the pinnace's engines rose and fell as the AI fought desperately to keep the ship on course. Silence accessed the instruments directly, and bit his lip as he saw they were still more than four minutes from Base Thirteen and the landing pads.

The pinnace's nose dropped sharply, as though some immense weight had settled upon it, outside. There was a screech of rending metal, and the port bulkhead tore like paper. Jagged rents surged down the wall, grouped together like giant claw-marks.

Something pounded against the outer hull, and great dents and bulges appeared in the cabin roof.

'There's nothing out there!' screamed Stasiak, beating blindly with his fists against the chair's armrests. 'There's nothing out there! The instruments say so!'

Ripper's head swayed back and forth, his mouth forming soundless denials. The Investigator glared about her at the fury of the storm, her hand clutching at the gun on her hip. Things were moving in the storm, dark and indistinct and impossibly huge. The whole frame of the pinnace groaned as the roof bulged inwards, forced down by some massive, intolerable weight.

'We're losing pressure, Captain,' said the AI quietly in Silence's ear. 'The ship's integrity has been breached beyond my ability to compensate. I am no longer confident of being able to reach the landing field. Do I have your permission to attempt an emergency landing?'

'No,' said Silence through his implant. 'Not yet.'

'We have to put down, before we fall apart!' said the Investigator.

Silence looked at her thoughtfully. He hadn't known she had access to the command channel. 'Not yet,' he said firmly. 'Esper; talk to them, damnit. Make them hear you!'

Diana Vertue dropped what remained of her mental shields and stood naked and defenceless before the alien presences. They rushed forward and swept over her. The pinnace punched through the last of the clouds and burst out into clear air. The metal trees swept towards and around the ship at dizzying speed. Vicious barbed spikes snapped past, seeming only inches away from tearing the pinnace open like a gutted fish. And then the trees too fell away, and they were flying over a vast open clearing, above a smooth and level plain, towards Base Thirteen and the landing pads.

'It's stopped,' said the Investigator quietly. 'Listen. It's stopped.'

Silence looked slowly around him. The pounding on the outer hull had ceased, and there was no trace anywhere of the dark, threatening presences. Faint creakings filled the pinnace as the ship's battered frame tried to repair itself. The two marines dropped out of fire control and looked blankly around them, seeing the damage for the first time. Ripper turned to the Captain for answers, but Silence waved for him to be quiet, and got out of his seat to kneel beside the esper, who was sitting slumped on the floor, head bowed.

She looked up slowly as she sensed his presence. 'They're gone, Captain. They just . . . left.'

'What did you see?' said Silence, keeping his voice calm and even with an effort.

'Faces. Gargoyle faces, all planes and angles. Teeth and jagged claws. I don't know. I don't think any of it was real. It couldn't have been. There were so many faces, and nothing in them but rage and hatred. I was sure they were going to kill me, but when I dropped my shields they just looked at me . . . and left. I don't know why.'

'But *you* do, Silence,' said the Investigator. 'Don't you?'

'Please return to your seats,' said the AI. 'I am preparing to land the pinnace.'

Silence helped the esper to her feet, and got her seated before returning to his own station. The Investigator scowled at his back for a moment, and then studiously ignored him. The marines looked at each other and said nothing, though their look spoke volumes.

'I have tried to contact Base Thirteen,' said the AI, 'but there is no response. The force Screen around the Base is still in operation, and there is no sign of life or movement anywhere within range of my sensors. I am therefore assuming it is safe to land, unless you wish to countermand me, Captain.'

'No, Odin. Set us down as close to the Base as you can. Then put your sensors on full alert, and maintain all weapons systems at battle status, until I tell you otherwise.'

'Understood, Captain.'

The pinnace slowed to a halt a dozen yards from the shimmering force Screen enclosing Base Thirteen, and settled gently on to the landing pad. Silence stared thoughtfully at the simulation covering the inner bulkheads, and for the first time was struck by the sheer size of the vast open space covered by the pads. The landing field had been intended originally to accommodate the massive starfreighters that built and established the Empire's Base. Silence had been the Captain of one of those ships, and he could still remember the constant flow of traffic around Base Thirteen as the ships came thundering in from all over the Empire. Huge silver ships had covered the landing pads for as far as the eye could see, like so many immense abstract sculptures. And now they were gone, and the pinnace stood alone on the pad, dwarfed by the size of the clearing and the towering trees that surrounded it.

He withdrew from the sensors, and the scene vanished, replaced by featureless steel walls. Silence turned in his chair and nodded abruptly to his team. 'I know you've all got a lot of questions, but you're going to have to bear with me for a while. The situation here is very complicated, and the rough ride we had on our way down is just the beginning. I take it no one's been badly injured? Good. Odin; damage reports.'

'Nothing important, Captain, but it'll be several hours before the ship can raise again. It's the hull breach that worries me most. There's a limit to what I can do, without access to a stardock's facilities.'

Silence nodded slowly. 'Worst-case scenario?'

'If I can't repair the hull, we're not going anywhere,

Captain. You could, of course, always call down another pinnace from the Darkwind, but there's no guarantee it would arrive here in any better condition than us.'

'Wait a minute,' said Stasiak. 'You mean we're stranded here?'

'Ease off,' said Ripper quickly. 'That was a worst-case scenario. Things aren't that bad. Yet.'

'I have some questions of my own, Captain,' said the Investigator coldly. 'This planet is officially listed as a scorched world. Nothing is supposed to live here any more. But something was trying to kill us in that storm, even if our sensors couldn't pick it up. And you know what it was. You recognised it. I represent the Empire in all matters concerning alien species, and I demand an explanation. What was that in the storm?'

'The Ashrai,' said Silence.

'But they're dead. Extinct.'

'Yes. I know. I told you the situation was complicated.'

'So what the hell was knocking the crap out of us on the way down?' said Stasiak. 'Ghosts?'

Silence smiled slightly. 'Perhaps. If ever a planet was haunted by its past, Unseeli is.' He hesitated, and looked quickly from one face to another. 'Did any of you ... feel anything, sense anything, on the way down?'

'Yeah,' growled Stasiak. 'I felt sure we were all going to be killed.'

Ripper shrugged. The Investigator scowled for a moment, and then shook her head. Silence looked at the esper. 'What about you, Diana? What did you sense?'

The young esper studied her hands, clasped tightly together in her lap. 'They could have killed us all. Our Screen couldn't keep them out, and our guns couldn't hurt them. But at the last moment they looked at me, and turned away. I don't know why. Do you know why, Captain?'

'Yes,' said Silence. 'Because you're innocent.' He raised a hand to forestall any further comments or questions. 'All right, pay attention. This was all put together in something of a hurry, so you haven't had much in the way of a briefing. That's at least partly because no one really knows what's going on here. And partly because I wanted you to come to this with open minds.

'Ten years ago, the Empire discovered that Unseeli was rich in important metals, and started mining operations. The main indigenous species, the Ashrai, objected strongly. They rose in rebellion against the Empire, aided by a traitor from within the Service; a man who turned against his own kind. The Empire troops were vastly outnumbered, and no match for the sheer ferocity of the Ashrai, even with their superior Empire weaponry. But they couldn't afford to lose. The metals were too important. So they retreated offworld, called in the starcruisers and scorched the whole damn planet from pole to pole. The metal trees survived unharmed. Nothing else did. Mining resumed soon after.

'But that's not all of the story. The trees are not just trees. They cover ninety per cent of the planet's surface, and are one hundred per cent metal. They contain no organic matter at all, but they are quite definitely alive. These trees were grown, not sculpted. Their roots draw metals from deep within the planet, separating out the heavy metals and storing them within their trunks. We don't know how they do this. There is reason to believe the trees were genetically engineered. Certainly it strains credulity that something so amazingly useful could have evolved entirely by chance. Especially when you consider that the particular heavy metals these trees store are ideally suited for powering a stardrive. Given how scarce such metals usually are, you can understand why the Empire was prepared to do absolutely anything to ensure that the mining of Unseeli's unique forest could continue uninterrupted.'

'Hold it,' said Frost. 'Are you saying the Ashrai created these trees?'

'No,' said Silence. 'Their civilisation was never that advanced. In fact, the original Investigating team uncovered evidence that suggested the Ashrai actually evolved long after the trees had first been planted.

Which gives you some idea of how long these trees have been here.'

'But if the Ashrai didn't genegineer the trees,' said Ripper slowly, 'who did?'

'Good question,' said Silence. 'Whoever it was, let's hope they don't come back to find out who's been messing with their garden. Now then; where was I? Ah yes; there are twenty substations on Unseeli, overseeing the automated mining machinery as it destroys the forest's roots, so that the trees can be easily felled and harvested. Base Thirteen oversees all the other substations, and is the only manned station on the planet. Its personnel spend most of their time sitting around waiting for something to go wrong so they can go out and fix it. They last communicated with the Empire four days ago. We haven't been able to get a word out of them since. At present, the situation is merely annoying, if a little disturbing. But if it continues, and the supply of metals slows as the mining machinery breaks down, the Empire could be in serious trouble. I'm afraid we've all become just a little too dependent on Unseeli's riches. Any questions so far?'

'Yes,' said Ripper. 'What are you doing here, Captain? It's not usual for a ship's Captain to expose himself to danger like this.'

'This is not a usual situation,' said Silence. 'And I have ... personal reasons for being here. Which I don't intend to discuss at this time.'

'All right,' said Frost. 'Let's talk about Base Thirteen instead. A force Screen is the last refuge for a Base under attack. What could possibly have threatened them so much, scared them so badly, that they had to retreat behind a Screen to feel safe?'

'Maybe they saw ghosts too,' said Diana Vertue.

Silence smiled briefly. 'When we get inside the Base, you can ask them.'

'And just how are we supposed to get inside?' said Frost sharply. 'We don't have anything powerful enough to break through a force Screen. The disrupter cannon on the *Darkwind* might do the job, but that kind of firepower would flatten everything inside a square mile, most definitely including everything and everyone inside the Screen. You'd be able to carry away what was left of Base Thirteen in a medium-sized bucket.'

'Right,' said Stasiak, scowling unhappily. 'There's only one way we're going to get past that Screen, and that's if someone inside the Base gets to the main command centre and shuts down the Screen. And that doesn't seem very likely, just at the moment. So, Captain, unless you have access to some kind of super-weapon the Empire has never heard of, we've come all this way for nothing.'

Silence looked at him calmly. 'Don't raise your voice to me, Stasiak, there's a good chap. I know what I'm doing. Computer; any hostile life signs outside the ship?'

'Negative, Captain,' said the AI promptly. 'There are no life signs anywhere within reach of my sensors. My files tell me that Base Thirteen has one hundred and twenty-seven personnel, but I regret I am unable to confirm that. The force Screen blocks my sensor probes.'

'What about the things that attacked us on the way down?' said Diana Vertue. 'They can't have just vanished.'

'My sensors detected no life signs at any time during the descent,' said the AI. 'If there had been any attackers, I would have detected them, and informed you of their nature. May I remind you, esper Vertue, this is a scorched world. Nothing lives here.'

'Well something beat the hell out of this ship on the way down,' said Frost. 'I can see some of the dents from here.'

'I agree that the pinnace has suffered extensive storm damage,' said the AI calmly. 'Nevertheless, I must insist that there were no life signs present in the storm. If there were, my instruments would have detected them.'

'I saw them with my esp,' said Diana. 'I felt their rage.'

'Hallucinations, perhaps,' said the AI. 'Possibly brought about by the stress of the descent. I can supply tranquillisers, if required.'

'Not just now,' said Silence. 'All right, people, get

ready to disembark. Full field kit for everyone, and
that includes you, esper. Move it!'

The pinnace crew rose quickly to their feet, and
gathered around the Investigator as she broke open
the arms locker and passed out the equipment. The
two marines looked at each other thoughtfully. Full
field kit meant a steel-mesh tunic, concussion and
incendiary grenades, swords and energy guns, and a
personal force shield. That kind of kit was normally
reserved for open fire-fights and full-scale riot control.
Stasiak took his armful of equipment and moved as
far away from the Captain and the Investigator as the
cramped space would allow. Ripper followed him,
and the two marines put their heads together as they
ostensibly busied themselves in sorting out their kit.

'I hate this,' said Stasiak quietly. 'I hate this planet,
and I hate this mission. Full field kit for what's
supposed to be a dead planet? A Captain who talks
about ghosts and super-weapons? The man is
seriously disturbed, Ripper. Damnit to hell, only five
more months and my time is up. Five short months,
and I'll be out of the Service and my own man again.
But of course nothing ever goes right for me, so I end
up being volunteered for this bloody mess. A crazy
Captain and an insane mission. Hallucinations, my
arse! I don't care if this is a scorched world; something's still alive here, and it isn't friendly.'

'Then why couldn't we find any targets for our
guns?' murmured Ripper, pulling on his baldric with

practised ease. 'There's no doubt this is a scorched world. I checked the ship's computers before the drop. Ten years ago, six starcruisers hit Unseeli with everything they had. Wiped the planet clean, pole to pole.'

'Six ships?' said Stasiak. 'Standard procedure for a scorching is two starcruisers, three if you're in a hurry. What did they have down here that they thought they needed six ships to deal with it?'

'There's more,' said Ripper. 'Guess who was in charge of scorching Unseeli?'

Stasiak stopped struggling with the buckles on his baldric. 'Silence?'

'Got it in one. He was in charge of putting down the Ashrai rebellion. When that got out of hand, he was the one who called for a scorch.'

Stasiak shook his head slowly. 'This just gets better and better. This is going to be a bad one, Rip. I can feel it in my water.'

'Don't worry; trust the old Ripper. He'll see you through.'

Stasiak just looked at him.

Esper Diana Vertue struggled to pull on her steel-mesh tunic. The label said it was her size, but the label was a liar. She finally pulled it into place by brute force, and emerged from the neck-hole red-faced and gasping. The long vest was heavy and awkward, and she hated to think what it was going to feel like after she'd been wearing it for a few hours.

She looked at the sword and the hand disrupter she'd been issued, hesitated, and then moved back to the arms locker to put them away.

'I wouldn't,' said Investigator Frost. 'The odds are you're going to need them.'

'I don't use weapons,' said the esper firmly. 'I'm not a killer. I'll keep the force shield, but that's all.'

The Investigator shrugged. 'It's your neck.' She settled her own holstered disrupter comfortably on her right hip, and drew a scabbarded sword from the arms locker. It was a long sword, definitely not regulation issue, and the Investigator slung it over her left shoulder and buckled it into place so that it hung down her back. The tip of the scabbard almost touched the floor behind her. Frost noticed the esper's curious gaze, and smiled slightly.

'It's a claymore. Old Earth sword. Been in my clan for generations. It's a good blade.'

'Have you ever killed anyone with it?' said Vertue. Her voice was polite, but the Investigator stiffened at the disapproval she sensed in the esper.

'Of course,' said Frost. 'That's my job.' She reached into the locker and brought out a bandolier of grenades. She pulled it tight across her chest and flexed her arms a few times to make sure it wouldn't interfere with her movements. She looked at the esper. 'If you're not willing to fight, stay out of my way. And don't expect me to look after you. That's not my job.'

She slammed the arms locker shut and moved over to the Captain and the two marines waiting at the airlock door. Vertue looked after her for a moment, but said nothing. She joined the others, her gaze on her feet. Silence looked them all over, raised an eyebrow at the esper's lack of weapons, and then keyed in the airlock door's Security codes. It hissed open, and Silence led the way in. The airlock was only just big enough to take them all, and when the door hissed shut behind them, the cramped space became disturbingly claustrophobic. Vertue hugged herself tightly to stop herself trembling. She'd never liked enclosed spaces.

'Odin, this is the Captain,' said Silence through his comm implant. 'Respond, please.'

'Contact confirmed,' murmured the AI in his ear. 'Sensor scans are still normal. No life forms within sensor range. Air, temperature and gravity are within acceptable limits. You have seven hours' daylight remaining.'

'Open the hatch, computer.'

The outer door swung open with a hiss of compressed air. Silence stepped forward, and then hesitated in the doorway as a breeze brought him the scent of Unseeli. It was a sharp, smoky scent, and though he hadn't smelt it for ten years, it was immediately familiar to him again, as if he'd never left. He lifted his head a little, and stepped on to the landing pad, followed by the others. The grey afternoon was bitter cold, and his breath steamed on the air before him. There was a series of faint clicks as the heating elements in his uniform kicked in. Tall metal trees surrounded the landing field, filling the horizon no matter which way he looked.

Base Thirteen stood in the centre of the landing field, hidden behind its force Screen. The protective dome swirled and shimmered, like a huge pearl in a dull metal setting. It was easy to imagine something dark and unknown squatting behind the Screen, staring out at the pinnace's crew and waiting for them to come to it. A sudden chill ran up Silence's spine that had nothing to do with the cold. He smiled sourly and shrugged the thought aside. He looked around to see what his people made of their new surroundings. The two marines had their disrupters in their hands, and were glancing quickly about them, checking for threats and familiarising themselves with the territory. The Investigator was standing calmly a little to one side, studying the force Screen thoughtfully. The esper was hugging herself against the cold and staring out at the forest, her eyes very large in her pale, bony face. None of them looked particularly worried. That would change, soon enough.

Silence coughed loudly to get their attention. 'I'm going to have to leave you for a while. The Investigator is in charge until I return. Any problems, she can contact me on the command channel. But unless it's vitally important, I don't want to be disturbed. We're

going to need help to get through that Screen, and I
think I know where to find some.'

Frost looked at him narrowly. 'Help? On Unseeli?
Don't you think it's about time you filled us in on
what's going on here, Captain?'

'No,' said Silence. 'Not just yet.'

'Well can you at least tell us where you're going?'

'Of course, Investigator. I'm going to talk to the
traitor called Carrion. He's going to get us through
the Screen. That's if he doesn't decide to kill us all
first.'

CHAPTER TWO

Ghosts

Ripper and Stasiak were supposed to be establishing a perimeter around the landing field, but they spent most of their time studying the enigmatic metal forest through the swirling mists. They had both volunteered for the job; Ripper because he believed in the value of a good secure perimeter, and Stasiak because he was glad of a chance to get away from the Investigator. He'd heard a lot of stories about the Empire's most renowned assassins, and now that he'd met Frost he was ready to believe a lot of things he hadn't before. Investigators were the Empire's élite, trained to tackle situations too dangerous or too complex for ordinary troops. Their speciality lay in dealing with new alien species. They would study the aliens in depth, work out how best to exploit, enslave or destroy them, and then lead the mission that would bring the alien world into the Empire, one way or another. They were unparalleled fighters, cold and calculating strategists, unstoppable by anything but death. They were said to be as strange and inhuman as the aliens they studied, and Stasiak believed it. Just being around Frost made his skin crawl.

The two marines moved slowly round the boundary of the landing pads, setting down proximity mines at regular intervals and priming them to detonate the moment anything approached within the designated distance. Ripper was a great believer in proximity mines; they not only discouraged people from sneaking up on you, they also provided plenty of warning that the enemy was abroad. Ripper slapped the mine before him affectionately, ignoring Stasiak's wince. They weren't much to look at, but there was enough explosive crammed into the flat grey discs to ruin anybody's day.

The perimeter had taken longer to establish than he'd expected, and not just because of the time they spent warily watching the forest. The landing field was even larger than it looked, and it looked immense. Ripper tried to picture how the field must have appeared when the Base was first being established, and the massive starcruisers were landing and taking off every hour, like huge flying mountains, but he couldn't. The scale was just too great. He started to mention it to Stasiak, but changed his mind. Stasiak was a good man to have at your back in a fight, but he wasn't the most imaginative of men. If you couldn't eat it, drink it, fight it or get a leg over it, Stasiak really wasn't interested. He was currently scowling out into the mists again, and Ripper reluctantly followed his gaze.

There was something about Unseeli in general and Base Thirteen in particular that disturbed Ripper deeply on some primitive, instinctive level. The sheer size of the metal trees was intimidating, making him feel small and insignificant, like a church mouse staring up at a vast cathedral. And then there was the mist, enveloping the metallic forest like a grubby off-white shroud. He kept thinking he saw vague shapes moving at the edge of the forest, come and gone in the blink of an eye. There was a constant feeling of being watched, an almost tangible pressure of unseen, watching eyes. Alien eyes.

The silence was unnerving too. The only sounds on the still air were those the two marines made themselves, and they were quickly swallowed up by the quiet. No creature roared, no bird sang, and the air had a deathly feel. Dead world. Ghostworld. Ripper scowled, and let his hand rest on the disrupter at his side while Stasiak finished laying down the last mine. There was a feeling of imminence, of something vital finally about to happen after many years of waiting. But all around, everything was at rest. Dead.

Stasiak ran quickly through the activating routine, primed the proximity mine, and stood up next to Ripper. Anyone approaching the perimeter without the right codes in their implant would find themselves suddenly scattered across an extremely large area. Stasiak sniffed unhappily, and hitched the gun on his hip to a more comfortable position. He'd hoped to feel more secure once the perimeter was established, but he couldn't honestly say that he did. One look at the forest was enough to put his teeth on edge. Strange colours glowed in the depths of the mists, curious and unsettling hues that swirled slowly like dye in water. They faded in and out, their slow deliberate movements implying something that bordered on purpose or meaning, some strange intent unfathomable by the human mind. Ripper tapped him on the arm to get his attention, and Stasiak all but jumped out of his skin. He glared meaningfully at Ripper, who stared calmly back.

'If you've quite finished trying to give me a coronary,' said Stasiak, 'perhaps we could get the hell away from here and back to the pinnace?'

Ripper looked at him in amusement. 'I thought you were relieved to be putting some distance between you and the big bad Investigator?'

Stasiak shrugged quickly, looking out at the forest again. 'I was, but this is even creepier than she is. I keep . . . seeing things. Hearing things. Come on, Rip; you've felt it too, I can tell. There's something out there in the mists, watching us.'

'The computer was quite specific,' said Ripper neutrally. 'According to all the pinnace's instruments, the only living things here are us. Unless you're suggesting the planet is haunted . . .'

'Why not?' said Stasiak, looking seriously at Ripper. 'Strange things have been known to happen out here, on the Rim. Remember the Ghost Warriors, and the Wolfling in the Madness Maze? You can find anything out here on the Rim. *Anything*.'

'Even so,' said Ripper, 'I still draw the line at ghosts.'

'Something attacked us on the way down, something the sensors swore wasn't there. And what about this Carrion guy the Captain's gone looking for? Assuming he isn't a ghost or a walking corpse, that means someone's found a way to hide from Empire sensors. And if one man's learned to do it, how do we know others haven't? A whole lot of others, heavily armed and just waiting to descend on us the moment we let our guard down.'

'You're determined to be cheerful, aren't you?' said Ripper. 'All right, I've got a bad feeling about this place too, but I'm not letting my nerves run away with me. I'm not going to start worrying till I've got something definite I can aim a gun at. You worry too much, Lou. These mines will stop anything, up to and including a charging Hadenman.'

'And if you're wrong, and there is something nasty out there?'

'Then you can say "I told you so",' said Ripper calmly.

Stasiak shook his head, unconvinced. 'There must have been something threatening here for the Base to raise their Screen. I mean, that's a last-ditch defence;

it's what you do when you've tried everything else and none of it's worked. I don't like this, Rip, I don't like the feel of this mission at all.'

'Neither do I,' said a calm female voice behind them. Both marines spun round sharply to find Investigator Frost standing almost on top of them. Ripper and Stasiak exchanged a swift glance as they realised neither of them had heard the Investigator approaching, despite the eerie quiet.

'There's still no response from the Base,' said Frost. 'There's nothing wrong with our equipment, so either the Base personnel don't want to talk to us, or they can't. Which suggests, at the very least, there's something here capable of scaring the hell out of an entire Base. Except, of course, our instruments continue to assure us there's no one down here but us.'

'What about Carrion?' said Stasiak, and the Investigator nodded slowly.

'Yes; what about Carrion? Have either of you heard the name before?'

'No,' said Ripper. 'Have you?'

Frost frowned thoughtfully. 'Most of Unseeli's records are sealed behind Security codes even I don't have access to, but I've managed to dig up a few things that aren't exactly common knowledge. The traitor Carrion used to be a high-ranking officer serving under Captain Silence, back when the Empire was fighting its war against the indigenous species, the Ashrai. Carrion turned against his own kind, and fought with the Ashrai, against humanity. Quite successfully, from what I can tell. He apparently displayed quite powerful esper abilities in combat, though interestingly enough there are no records of his having any such abilities before he came to Unseeli. He was supposed to have perished with the Ashrai, when the planet was scorched.'

Stasiak shook his head firmly. 'Then he's dead. No one survives a scorching.'

'Not so far,' said Frost. 'But the Captain seems quite convinced that Carrion *has* survived, and that he can find him. Intriguing, that.'

'Have you ever served with Captain Silence before?' said Ripper.

'No. He has a good record, apart from Unseeli. How about you?'

'Been with him two years now,' said Ripper. 'Not a bad sort. For a Captain. I've served under worse. Lou?'

'He's all right,' said Stasiak, shrugging. 'Or at least he seemed to be, until this mission. He's been acting strangely ever since we got our orders to come here.'

'Considering the last time he was here he fouled up so completely he had to have the whole planet scorched, I can't say I'm surprised.' Frost looked thoughtfully at the metallic forest, as though it might suggest some answers. 'I would have to say the good Captain's present behaviour could become a cause for concern. In fact, he gives the definite impression of a man no longer entirely stable.'

Ripper looked at her sharply. The Investigator was choosing her words very carefully. 'So,' he said, equally carefully. 'If the Captain was to be officially judged as unstable, who would take over as mission commander? You?'

The Investigator smiled. 'I might. For the good of the mission.'

'I should remind you all,' said the AI suddenly through their comm implants, 'the penalties for treason and mutiny are extremely severe.'

'Treason?' said Stasiak quickly. 'Who's talking treason? I'm not.'

Frost smiled, unperturbed. Ripper grimaced sourly. 'I should have known. Can't even get any privacy on a deserted planet.'

'I am required in the present emergency to monitor all conversations,' said the AI. 'I shall of course have to repeat your words to the Captain, on his return.'

'Of course,' said Frost. 'When he returns. In the meantime, you will cease to monitor any conversation of which I am a part, unless I give you permission to do so. That is a direct order, under Code Red Seven. Confirm.'

'Code Red Seven confirmed,' said the AI, almost reluctantly, and then it fell silent.

Ripper raised an eyebrow at the Investigator. 'I didn't know anyone could override an AI's Security directives.'

'That's what's so special about a career in the

Service,' said Frost. 'You learn something new every day. Now, much as I'd like to stay and chat, I think I'll go for a little walk in the woods. Get the feel of this place. If you feel the need to discuss the Captain again, I suggest you wait till my return.'

She strode off towards the metallic forest without looking back, and the marines watched silently until she'd disappeared into the curling mists. Stasiak looked at Ripper. 'You know, I'm not sure which disturbs me most; this planet, or her.'

Silence made his way unhurriedly through the mists, looking always straight ahead of him. The huge trees loomed out of the fog to every side, and once-familiar faces seemed to appear at the corners of his eyes, but he never looked round. The forest was full of old memories, few of them pleasant. Silence concentrated on the man he'd come to find, the traitor called Carrion. The man who'd been his friend, ten long years ago.

The heating elements in his uniform kept his body comfortably warm, but the bitter cold seared his bare hands and face. The Empire kept promising to supply gloves to go with the uniform, but somehow the budget was always too tight, this year. He grimaced stoically, and did his best to ignore the cold. He wasn't far from his destination now. Theoretically, Carrion could be anywhere on Unseeli, shielded from the pinnace's sensors by his unnatural esper abilities. He had a whole world to hide in, but Silence knew where he'd be. Carrion was waiting for him in the clearing half a mile from the landing field, the place where Carrion had lived with the Ashrai in their tunnels under the earth, and called it home.

He stopped for a moment, and activated his comm implant. 'Carrion; this is John Silence, Captain of the Darkwind. Can you hear me?' He waited, but there was no reply. He wasn't surprised. Carrion wasn't stupid enough to give himself away that easily. Anyone could be listening in on an open comm channel, and he knew it.

Something moved suddenly at the edge of Silence's vision, and he snapped round, disrupter in hand. There was nothing there, but Silence had a strong feeling that something had been. Whatever had attacked the pinnace during its descent had found him again. There were sharp darting movements in the mists to his left and right, behind and ahead of him. Silence started forward again, careful to keep his pace slow and unhurried. He felt a growing need to break into a run, away from the shadows that were moving inexorably closer, but he didn't. It wouldn't be wise for them to get the idea he was running from them. It wouldn't be safe. He wasn't far from the clearing now. It occurred to him that they might not want him to meet Carrion, and the first stab of uncertainty brought beads of sweat to his face despite the cold. He had to reach Carrion. He had to.

Glowing streamers of quickly changing hues spun in the mists ahead of him, pushed and tugged by an unfelt wind. There was a sudden sharp crack as a long metal branch snapped off a nearby tree. The jagged spike slammed into the ground where Silence had been standing as he threw himself to one side. Cracking sounds echoed from every side as more branches broke off from the trees, raining down about him as he dodged and ducked down the path towards the clearing. His boots thudded hard on the unyielding ground, jarring him painfully. He threw himself this way and that, lungs straining against the cold air, and the metal spears slammed into the ground all around him. Silence refused to be slowed or intimidated. He'd come too far to be stopped now. A jagged spike tore through his uniform and slid painfully across his ribs before falling away. He thought he'd got away with only a bruise, until he glanced down and saw the wide patch of blood staining his side. Another spike flew at his face, and he deflected it at the last moment with an upraised arm. Blood flew on the air as the uniform sleeve tore, and the impact numbed his arm.

There were things in the forest now, moving with him. He could hear them pounding between the trees, the ground shaking from their weight. Silence plunged on, his breath burning in his heaving chest. His gun was still in his hand, but he couldn't see a target anywhere. And then the path ended suddenly, blocked by a clump of needle-thorned briar that had grown up around a fallen tree. Silence staggered to a halt, and dropped to his knees by the massive trunk of a golden tree. He put his back to the trunk and glared wildly about him. The briar blocked the way completely, and there was no other path. They had him now.

Deep in the metallic forest, something howled. It was a harsh, alien sound with nothing human in it, but the pain and rage of remembered loss were clear enough. The horrid noise drifted through the trees, growing louder, drawing nearer. More voices rose on every side, the deafening chorus cutting at Silence like a knife, and he shrank back against the tree trunk even as he raised his gun in a futile gesture of defiance. Guns weren't going to stop what was coming for him. Shadows moved in the swirling mists, encircling him, and Silence caught brief glimpses of clawed hands and snarling mouths, large graceful forms and flat-planed gargoyle faces.

He took aim and fired his disrupter. The crackling energy beam smashed through the nearest face and shattered the tree trunk behind it. There was a loud rending sound as the tree toppled slowly over and crashed to the forest floor. Metallic shrapnel pattered down for some time, but there was nothing to show he'd hurt or even scared his enemy. He hadn't really expected anything else. His enemies were already dead; ten years dead. They just wouldn't admit it and lie down. Silence's mouth twitched. They weren't playing fair. Not playing by the rules. Except this was Unseeli, the world of the Ashrai, and they had their own rules.

They were all around him now, the unearthly howls rising and falling till his head ached from them. He knew what had come for him, even though it made a mockery of all sense and reason. The Ashrai were moving slowly, steadily, through the mists and trees, circling, circling, all the tortured souls he'd damned and destroyed ten years earlier. Haunting him now as the memory of the awful thing he'd done had haunted him for so many years.

The howling stopped, cut off sharply between one moment and the next, and an eager, expectant hush filled the forest. Silence struggled to sit up a little straighter, grimacing briefly as pain flared in his damaged ribs. He raised his gun and then lowered it again. Even if there'd been anything to aim at, the disrupter couldn't fire again till its energy crystal had had time to recharge. There was still the sword at his side, but all he could do with that was fall on it himself, and maybe cheat the Ashrai of their vengeance. Except he couldn't do that. It wasn't in his nature to give up, even when the situation seemed hopeless. He drew his sword awkwardly, and sneered unyieldingly at his surroundings. Something moved in the forest, not far away. Not far away at all.

And then a man appeared suddenly out of the mist

to stand at Silence's side. Everything was still, the Captain's fate hanging in the balance, and then the pressure of countless watching eyes was gone in a moment, the mists and the forest empty, as though they always had been. Silence let out his breath in a long, shuddering sigh, and put his sword down beside him. He wiped the sweat out of his eyes with his sleeve and looked up at the man standing over him. The dark figure was tall and whipcord lean, dressed in black leather and a billowing black cape. Carrion always wore black, like the bird of ill omen he was. He was carrying a long staff of polished bone, almost as tall as himself, but he held it more like a weapon than an aid to walking. His face was hidden in the shadows of his cape's cowl, and Silence didn't know whether to feel grateful for that or not.

'Hello, Sean,' he said finally, and was relieved to find his voice was still calm and even. 'It's been a long time.' The figure stared silently down at him, and Silence stirred uneasily. 'What's the matter? Don't you remember me?'

'Oh yes, Captain,' said Carrion quietly. 'I remember you. So do they.'

'What are they?' said Silence.

'The past. Ghosts, perhaps.'

'I don't believe in ghosts.'

'That's all right,' said Carrion. 'They believe in you.'

CHAPTER THREE

Looking for Answers

Stasiak and Ripper lounged bonelessly in their seats, bored and restless, watching without much interest as the esper Diana Vertue tried to make contact with Base Thirteen's computers. She'd been trying to patch the *Darkwind*'s computers into the Base's systems for some time, with only limited success, and she'd begun to mutter under her breath. Finally, by working together and improvising madly, she and the AI Odin had managed to forge a tentative link between the pinnace's onboard systems and the Base's computer net. Diana studied the incoming data closely, and winced at the state of the Base's systems as they reluctantly opened up to her tentative probes. Thirteen's computers were shot to hell. Half the main systems had crashed, and there was no trace anywhere of the Base's AI, which was supposed to protect the systems from such devastation. And there was something definitely odd about the computers she had managed to reach.

Diana frowned, her fingers darting across the comm panels, and watched intently as one by one the pinnace's monitors came to life, information flowing in an endless stream across the glowing screens. Her fingers pecked and stabbed at the keyboard as she tried to sort out the important data from the dross, her frown deepening as the picture unfolded. Whatever had happened at Base Thirteen, it hadn't been an accident. This kind of selective damage had to have been deliberate. Though whether the attack had come from outside the Base or within had yet to be established. She half smiled as she heard one of the marines sigh heavily behind her. It was probably Stasiak. He hadn't struck her as the type to have a long attention span.

'You don't have to stay, you know,' she said briskly, without looking back. 'There's nothing you can do to help.'

'It's our job to look after you,' said Stasiak. 'Make sure nothing happens to you. And if that means sitting around in a nice warm cabin instead of tramping around in the cold, waiting for my extremities to drop off, well, I know where my duty lies. After all, with the Captain and the Investigator both wandering about on their own somewhere, Rip and I are all that stands between you and whatever horrors lie waiting out there in the trees. Right, Rip?'

'Right,' said Ripper.

'The proximity mines are all the protection I need,' said Diana. 'And the pinnace does have its own force Screen, in the event of a real emergency. Now, I'm going to be doing this for some time, and believe me, this is as interesting as it gets.'

'How much progress have you made?' said Ripper, and Diana gave him credit points for at least sounding like he was interested.

'Not a hell of a lot,' she admitted, sitting back in her chair and letting her fingers rest for a moment. Things would have been going a lot quicker if she'd been allowed direct access to the computers like the Captain, instead of having to work through the keyboard. But she wasn't high enough in rank for that privilege, and besides, she was an esper, and therefore not to be trusted. Ever. She realised Ripper was still waiting for her answer, and pulled herself together.

'Most of the Base's computers are off line, and seem determined to stay that way, no matter what I do. They're not responding to the standard code words or entry routines, and I can't even find the Base's AI. If I didn't know better, I'd swear it was hiding. It's as though someone or something just shut everything down, and then wiped half the memory crystals. The subsystems overseeing the mining machinery seem to be mostly intact, but what little information I'm getting from them is pretty depressing. The machinery is working at barely twenty-percent efficiency, and dropping. Unless we come up with something to reverse this process, or at least slow it down, everything will just grind to a halt in a little under forty-eight hours. And once they've

stopped it'll be hell's own problem to get them all
started again. If that were to happen, the Empire
would not be at all happy; and guess which three
people sitting in this cabin right now would be most
likely to be saddled with the blame.'

'Is there anything we can do to help?' said Ripper.

'Short of getting me into the Base so I can get my
hands on the main computer terminals, no, not
really. Odin is working its electronic nuts off trying to
find a way into the main computers, but something
down here is playing merry hell with our comm
signals, which means Odin isn't working at anywhere
near full capacity.

'On top of all that, the information I have been
getting makes no sense at all. Half is just gibberish,
and the rest is impossible. If I didn't know better, I'd
swear some of these systems have been repro-
grammed from the bottom up.'

Stasiak and Ripper looked at each other, and Ripper
leaned forward in his seat. 'Are you saying someone
within the Base could have crashed the systems
deliberately?'

'Yes. I'd have to say that was a definite possibility.'

'In which case,' said Ripper slowly, 'we could be
dealing with enemy action.'

'Maybe,' said Diana. 'I can't say for sure. Some of
these changes make no sense at all.'

Ripper got to his feet. 'Lou; I think you and I had

better take a stroll round the perimeter. Make sure everything's secure.'

Stasiak leaned back in his seat and deliberately stretched out his legs. 'Come on, Rip, have a heart. It's cold out there. I'm rather attached to my fingers and toes and I'd like to hang on to them. You take a walk, if you feel like it. I'm sure Diana and I can come up with something to keep us occupied while you're gone. Right, Diana?'

'In your dreams,' said the esper calmly. 'You're not my type, Lou. I usually prefer my men a little higher up the evolutionary scale.'

'Can I take that as a maybe?' said Stasiak, getting reluctantly to his feet.

'Think of it more as a get the hell out of here.'

'All right,' said Stasiak. 'I can take a hint. Lead the way, Rip. I'm just dying to take a nice little stroll in sub-zero temperatures, and watch my extremities turn blue.'

The esper chuckled briefly, intent on the comm panels, but she didn't relax until she heard the airlock door close behind the two marines. Stasiak was all right, in his way, but she had to be careful whom she allowed to get close to her. There were always people ready to try and take advantage of her esper abilities. But it wasn't safe to stay unattached, either. Espers always had a need for someone to stand between them and the Empire; someone strong enough to protect a second-class citizen like an esper from official displeasure and political pogroms. Stasiak was too far down the ladder to be any use to her, and Ripper wasn't much better ... She realised her thoughts were drifting, and made herself concentrate on the screens before her. The information from Base Thirteen's computers flowed endlessly on, much of it strange and enigmatic and no bloody use to her at all.

'I'm picking up something ... unusual,' said Odin suddenly. 'I thought at first it was what was left of the Base's AI, but now I'm not sure. It's as though something inside the Base is trying to respond to my enquiries, but in a manner unlike anything I've ever encountered before.'

'Put it on the main screen,' said Diana, and then frowned thoughtfully as the AI showed her a record of its questions and the Base's responses. The answers were garbled and obscure, bordering on the edge of meaning without actually achieving it. Diana ran a few simple checks to see if the gibberish might contain some kind of code, but if so, it was buried so deep she couldn't find it. And yet the words continued to nag at her, trying to tell her ... something. 'Run a full analysis on this, Odin,' she said finally. 'Look for repetition of words and phrases, subjects emphasised or avoided; all the usual things. If it isn't the AI, could it be someone alive, inside the Base?'

'If it is,' said Odin, 'I would have to say that they were quite insane.'

*

Outside the pinnace, it was even colder than Stasiak remembered, and he hugged himself tightly, and stamped his feet hard on the landing pad while he waited for the heating elements in his uniform to kick in. He was beginning to think he should have found the time to give his uniform a thorough overhaul before he came down here. It was long overdue, and Stasiak was coming to the conclusion he might have left it a little too long. He shrugged, and rubbed his hands together briskly. He'd survive. Ripper, of course, was taking no notice of the cold, and was staring out at the forest boundary with calm, thoughtful eyes. Stasiak followed his gaze, but was damned if he could make out anything significant, or even interesting. He sniffed loudly, and looked longingly back at the pinnace.

'Ripper; tell me you didn't just drag me out here for the exercise. Tell me there's a good reason why I'm standing here in the cold, before I decide to batter you to death with a blunt instrument, and dance a jig on your remains.'

'You don't have a blunt instrument,' said Ripper, without looking round.

'I'll improvise!'

Ripper smiled, but still didn't look away from the forest. 'You weren't looking at the sensor panels, were you? According to the sensors built into our proximity mines, something or someone has approached or crossed our perimeter in several places, before falling back to the forest again.'

'You're kidding,' said Stasiak. 'You've got to be kidding. If something's crossed our perimeter, why haven't the mines gone off?'

'Good question,' said Ripper. 'Another good question might be why did the mines' sensors detect a presence, when the pinnace's instruments continue to insist there are no living things on this planet apart from us. You've got to admit, Lou; it's an interesting place our Captain has brought us to.'

'I'll give him "interesting",' said Stasiak darkly. He moved over to stand beside Ripper, and glared out at the distance. 'You know why he brought us here, Rip? Because we're expendable. We're just here to test the water for him. And if anything were to happen to us, he'd just shrug and say what a pity, and then contact the Darkwind and have them ship down two more warm bodies.'

'That goes with the job,' said Ripper. 'With being a marine. If you can't take a joke, you shouldn't have joined.'

'Just let me survive the next five months, and my contract will be up,' said Stasiak. 'And then I'll be out of the marines so fast it'll make your head spin. I still can't believe I landed an assignment like this so close to getting free of it all. I'll tell you this for nothing, Rip; I'm not taking a single risk down here that I don't absolutely have to. I'm taking this one by the book and by the numbers, with no volunteering for anything. Whatever else happens on this mission, I am coming back alive and intact, and you can put money on that.'

Ripper finally turned to look at him. 'And what will you do then, Lou? Where will you go, once you've left the Service? All you know, all your training and experience, comes from being a marine. There aren't that many openings for a professional killer, outside the Service. Shall I tell you what's going to happen to you? You'll go from one dead-end job to another, each more frustrating than the one before, breaking your back every day for half the money you used to make as a marine. And finally, when your money's run out, and you're out of your mind with boredom, some shark with a big smile and a suit that cost a year of your wages will sign you up as a mercenary, for which he gets a nice commission, and you get to tour the hell spots of the Empire. In the end you'll come running back to the Service and sign on again, just like most ex-marines do.'

'Like you did,' said Stasiak.

'Yeah. Like I did. Get used to the idea, Lou. This is all there is, for people like us.'

'Not me,' said Stasiak. 'Once I'm out of here they're never getting their hands on me again. I've got plans. I'm going places. I'm going to make something of myself.'

'Sure you are, Lou.'

'I mean it!'

'I know you do. I hope you make it. In the meantime, keep your eyes open and your head down. And
don't look now, but I think I just saw something
moving out on the perimeter, at two o'clock.'

Stasiak looked round casually, his eyes just happening to drift past two o'clock. There was nothing there.
He cut in his infra-red implants, but no heat traces
showed anywhere on the perimeter. He patched into
the pinnace sensors and studied their signals directly,
but there was still nothing anywhere on the boundary. He dropped out of contact, looked at Ripper,
and shrugged.

'Jumping at shadows, Rip. There's nothing out
there.'

'Yes there is. I saw it. Keep watching; it'll give itself
away. It's at times like this I wish the Empire would
relax its ban on all but the most essential implants.
I've seen stuff on the black market you wouldn't
believe; implants and built-in weapon systems that
could make a man unbeatable in the field. Which is
pretty much why they're banned, of course. The
Empire doesn't want its good little soldier boys
getting ideas above their station. They still haven't
forgotten the Hadenman rebellion.'

'Yeah well,' said Stasiak. 'Those cyborgs were
enough to frighten anyone. And I still can't see
anything out there. Maybe it's the Captain, on his way
back.'

'If it was, he'd have shown up on the infra red, wouldn't he? Though that is another question worth thinking about. What is the good Captain doing down here, risking his precious neck dirtside with grunts like us?'

'Looking for Carrion, whoever he is.'

'Yeah.' Ripper frowned for the first time. 'The Captain knows a lot more about what's going on here than he's letting on. I'll lay you odds this Carrion turns out to be some kind of powerful esper. That's the only way he could be shielding himself from the pinnace's sensors.'

Stasiak shook his head dubiously. 'I don't know. If Carrion's been here on his own for the past ten years, what's he been living on? I mean; there isn't any game for him to catch. Every living thing was wiped out by the scorching. And even if he did find some way to survive, he's got to be stone crazy after ten years of his own company.'

'Not necessarily,' said Ripper. 'He could have worked out some kind of deal with the Base personnel. There! Did you see that?'

'Yeah,' said Stasiak quietly. 'Right at the edge of the forest; two o'clock, just like you said. Still can't make out what it is. Want to go and take a look?'

'Easy, Lou. It could be a trick, to draw us away from the ship. Besides, if it's come this close, why hasn't it set off any of the mines? Whatever that is has got to be within their range. Maybe it's got a way to turn them on and off. It could be just waiting for us to walk by one, and then detonate it itself. Whoosh bang, and they'll send your balls home in a box, because they couldn't find the rest of you. No, Lou; short of an actual target or a direct threat to the pinnace, I'm not moving from this spot. At least, not until I've got a much better idea of the opposition.'

'Damn right,' said Stasiak, still keeping a careful if unobtrusive watch on two o'clock. 'If the Captain wants to go off on his own chasing after ghosts, that's his affair. Short of a direct order, I'm not moving. I can't see it any more, Rip. Can you see it?'

'No. It's gone again.'

Stasiak looked at the watch face imbedded in his wrist. 'The Captain's been gone a long time. He should have been back by now.'

Ripper shrugged. 'How long does it take to track down someone who officially doesn't exist? Don't worry about the Captain. He's a grown man. He can take care of himself.'

They stood together for a while, staring out into the mists.

'You know,' said Stasiak finally, 'if there was a ghost or something out there at two o'clock, that puts it in roughly the same sector as the Investigator. Perhaps they'll bump into each other.'

'In which case,' said Ripper, 'I feel sorry for the ghost.'

CHAPTER FOUR

Carrion

Captain Silence rose slowly to his feet, wincing despite himself as his injured ribs protested. Carrion made no move to help him, for which Silence was thankful. He didn't want any reason to feel grateful to Carrion. It would have made what he had to do that much harder. He pushed his various aches and pains to the back of his mind, and concentrated on the traitor called Carrion. It had been ten years since he'd last seen the man who used to be his friend, and he'd never expected to see him again. He should have died with the Ashrai. Dead, he might have emerged as a martyr; alive, he was just another loose end, an embarrassment. Someone Silence could use to solve an awkward problem.

He realised he was just standing and staring at Carrion, but the words wouldn't come. He'd had it all worked out, on the pinnace, coming down. He knew exactly what to say, what buttons to push to manipulate Carrion into doing what was necessary. Only now he was face to face with an old friend, a ghost from the past, and the words were ashes in his

mouth. This man had been closer than a brother, but
the last time they'd met they'd tried to kill each other.
For a long time, Silence believed he'd succeeded.
And then he began to hear stories from men who'd
served on Unseeli; stories of the man who wouldn't
die. The ghost in the trees. Carrion.

The years passed, but Silence never went back. He
didn't want to have to kill his friend again. But time
and circumstance had brought him back anyway, and
past sins belonged in the past. All that mattered now
was his mission, and the things he had to do to carry
it out. Silence knew his duty. He'd always known his
duty. And if that meant using and betraying his friend
one more time, he could live with that. He'd lived
with worse.

Carrion reached up and pushed back the cowl that
concealed his face. Silence felt a sudden chill run
through him, and the hackles rose on the back of his
neck. Carrion hadn't aged. He'd spent ten years alone
in terrible conditions, but there wasn't a single line
on his face. He looked just as Silence remembered
him; young, proud, unyielding. Time had not
touched him. But then, ghosts didn't age. Silence felt
suddenly awkward, ashamed at the changes that had
taken place in himself over the past decade. What did
Carrion make of him, with his retreating hairline and
his thickening waist? Had he even noticed, and if he
had, did he care? And most important, did he realise
that this was not the same John Silence he'd once

known, who might have hesitated to sacrifice his friend if the game demanded it? Just looking at the calm young man before him, Silence felt older, dirtier and more used. He still didn't know what to say. And in the end, Carrion was the one who broke the silence.

'What are you doing here, Captain?'

'I need your help,' said Silence evenly.

Carrion smiled briefly, as though it was something he'd lost the habit of, over the years. 'I didn't think you'd come all this way just to renew old acquaintance. I always knew you'd be back someday. We have unfinished business, you and I.'

'That can wait,' said Silence. 'Do you know what's happened in Base Thirteen?'

'I know the Screen went up, some time back. That's all.'

'You didn't have any contact with the Base personnel?'

The smile came and went again, but it didn't touch Carrion's eyes. 'The Base Commander had a shoot-on-sight policy where I was concerned. He needn't have bothered. He had nothing I wanted. But they were scared of me, of what I'd become, and they were right about that, at least.'

'What have you become?' said Silence. 'How have you survived here all these years, with no supplies and no resources?'

'Strictly speaking, I didn't. I've been through a lot

since we last met, Captain. I'm not the man you remember.' He looked away for a moment, as though listening to a voice only he could hear, and then nodded slowly and looked back at Silence. 'We can't talk here. You have no friends among the trees, and not even I can protect you against the whole of the forest. Come with me. My home isn't far.'

He turned and walked away, without once looking back to see if Silence was following. Silence moved off after him, gritting his teeth against the grinding pain in his side. The wound didn't look too severe, but something would have to be done about it soon, before he became weakened through blood loss. He allowed his uniform to release endorphins into his system, enough to handle the pain but not enough to cloud his thinking. He walked beside Carrion through the bronze and golden forest, following a track only the outlaw could see. Nothing moved in the mists, but the quiet had a sullen, expectant feel, and Silence could sense the watching eyes even if he couldn't see them.

The trees widened out suddenly to reveal a great hill of metal, overgrown with silver briar. The metal was scarred and pockmarked, and briar penetrated the outer shell here and there like some parasitic ivy, but even so Silence could still recognise the battle wagon beneath. There were supposed to be quite a few of them, scattered throughout the forest, left to lie where they had fallen, brought down by the Ashrai and their psi-storms. Silence thought he remembered the clearing; it was one of the few battlegrounds where he and Carrion had both been present.

Lasers flamed on the night, and concussion grenades blossomed in the dark like scarlet flowers. Disrupters flared, and there was the loud humming of raised force shields. The Ashrai came in never-ending waves, huge, ugly figures that moved with surprising grace and speed. Their psi-storms crackled on the air around them, altering probabilities and tearing at the mental barriers the Empire espers had cast over the ground troops. Claws and fangs met swords and shields, and blood flowed in rivers on the broken ground. Battle wagons lumbered through the night, forcing their way between the trees, and disrupter beams stabbed down from low-flying skimmers darting back and forth overhead. Science clashed with savagery, and the battle swept this way and that, neither side able to gain the upper hand for long.

Silence shivered suddenly, emerging from a memory so real it seemed to him that he could still hear the shouts and battle cries and the screams of the dying. The Ashrai had been a brave and cunning foe, but they never stood a chance against the Empire. As soon as Silence had realised he couldn't take the ground the Ashrai held, or hang on to his own, he simply moved all his people off planet and called in the starcruisers to scorch the whole damned planet from pole to pole. Millions died, all life was swept away, and not even the bodies remained to mark the fallen. The Empire was nothing if not thorough. Silence had won, and all it cost him was his honour and his friend. For a while he thought he'd die without them, but he didn't. No one ever really dies from a broken heart.

When it was over, the Empire hadn't really known what to do with Silence. On the one hand, he'd lost control of the situation, and had to be rescued by a scorching, but on the other hand, he had solved the Unseeli problem quite conclusively. And permanently. So they smiled and shook his hand and patted him on the head in public, and made a note on his file that he was never to be promoted. He could keep his Captaincy, but there'd never be anything more for him. Silence didn't care. He'd lost all taste for ambition on Unseeli.

And now here he was, back again, and it seemed the problem hadn't been solved after all.

They finally came to the clearing where Carrion had his home, and Silence was struck with an almost overpowering sense of *déjà vu*. It hadn't changed at all. Before him were the same trees, the same clearing, the same patch of metal briar camouflaging the trap-door entrance to the tunnels under the earth. Silence watched numbly as Carrion carefully lifted the briar to one side, and pulled open the trapdoor. The last time Silence had been here was when he'd made a last-minute trip against orders to try and talk Carrion out of turning traitor. They were still friends then, and the outlaw had yet to come by his new name. They'd met as friends and parted as enemies, and what happened afterward had all the inevitability of destiny. It hadn't stopped either of them from playing their rôle to the full. And now here they were again, with only the echoes of old friendship and enmity holding them together, looking once more for some middle ground they could agree on. Silence smiled sourly. Maybe they'd be luckier this time.

Carrion descended into the dark stairway the trapdoor had revealed, and Silence followed him down. He paused briefly to test the weight of the trapdoor. It was just as heavy as he'd remembered, but Carrion had hefted it with one hand, as though it was weightless. He cleared his throat, and Carrion looked up at him.

'Do you want me to shut the trapdoor behind us?' said Silence.

Carrion smiled briefly. 'There's really no need. It's not as if there was anyone else who might come in after us. Still, if it makes you feel more secure . . .'

He gestured at the trapdoor, and it started to lean slowly forwards. Silence hurried down the narrow earth steps into the gloom of the tunnel, and the trapdoor slammed shut behind him, the impact of its weight sending tremors through the earth walls and floor. Silence glared after Carrion, but he was already walking off down the tunnel, and Silence had to hurry to keep up. The tunnel was wide enough for both of them to walk side by side, with a good two or three-foot clearance above their heads. The earth had a rich, peaty smell that was not unpleasant. Roots from the metal trees had been trained along the uneven ceiling, filling the tunnel with their warm unwavering light. The enclosed space was still distinctly claustrophobic, and Silence tried hard not to think about the increasing weight of earth above him as the tunnel sloped steadily downwards.

It soon branched into two, and then in two again, with corridors leading off tunnels, and wide holes opening into vast, brightly lit caverns. Silence was soon lost in the labyrinth of tunnels that had been the home of the Ashrai and the outlaw Carrion. The last time he'd been down here, he and Carrion had still been friends enough that Carrion had led him back to the surface once their business was concluded. Silence wasn't sure if that was the case any more, but it didn't matter anyway. He had to talk to Carrion.

Finally the outlaw stopped by a side passage and waved for Silence to go in ahead of him. Silence stepped forward without hesitating. He didn't want Carrion to think he was intimidated. The passage widened out into a fair-sized cavern, lit by the ubiquitous glowing roots curling in the earth ceiling. Carrion's home was large enough to give the illusion of space, yet still cluttered with enough little comforts to make it seem almost cosy. There were two chairs, a writing table and a length of bedding. A banked fire muttered drowsily in one wall, the smoke rising up through a narrow chimney cut into the earth above. The floor was covered with some kind of woven matting, scuffed and stained with the marks of long usage. Not much of a place to spend an exile in.

Small, delicate Ashrai carvings filled discreet niches in the walls. Silence moved over to study the nearest, but its shape made no sense, and its twistings and turnings made his head ache. He looked away, frowning, and Carrion chuckled softly.

'You're supposed to touch them, Captain, not look at them. The Ashrai were a very tactile race, and their eyes were different than ours.'

'Thanks,' said Silence. 'I'll pass.'

'As you wish. Take a seat, Captain. Make yourself comfortable. I'd offer you a drink or a smoke, but I don't have any.'

Silence sank cautiously into the nearest chair, but it was tougher than it looked, and held his weight easily. Carrion dropped into the chair opposite, and the two men sat facing each other for a while. Silence couldn't get over how little Carrion had changed. Ten years of living alone hadn't put a dent in his composure. The outlaw was as infuriatingly polite as ever. After a decade of solitude he should have been falling all over Silence, desperate for the sound of a human voice. Instead he just sat there calmly, apparently quite happy to wait for whatever Silence had come to say to him. Silence stirred uneasily in his chair. He'd forgotten how cold and piercing Carrion's eyes could be.

'Nice place you have here,' he said finally, just to be saying something.

'I like it,' said Carrion. He leaned forward suddenly, and Silence jumped a little in spite of himself. Carrion didn't smile. 'I don't know what to say to you, Captain. It's been a long time since I spoke to another human being.'

'How have you managed to survive here on your own for ten years?' said Silence.

Carrion raised an eyebrow. 'Is it as long as that? I'd lost count. I survived by changing, adapting. By becoming more than human.'

'You look human enough to me,' said Silence. 'You've hardly changed at all.'

'That's Unseeli for you. Appearances can be deceiving. You should know that. You never did understand the Ashrai. They're what kept me alive all these years.'

Silence looked at him thoughtfully. 'Are you saying some of the Ashrai survived after all, hidden down here in the tunnels?'

'No, Captain. The Ashrai are extinct. You were very thorough. All the Ashrai are dead, and none but I am left to tell the tale. I survived because I was afraid to die. I've had a long time to consider whether that was a mistake or not. Why have you come back, Captain?'

'Things have changed since we last met.'

'Not for me. The Ashrai are still dead, and the

Empire machines are still burrowing away, tearing through the trees' roots so they can be felled and harvested. The rape of the planet goes on, day by day.'

Silence sighed tiredly. 'Ten years of solitude haven't done much to change your arguments. You didn't listen then and you probably won't now, but I'll try again anyway, for old times' sake. The Empire needs the metals it takes from Unseeli. Each tree that's felled can provide enough heavy metals to power a starship for a year. We even use the outer metals to make ships' hulls and engine casings. It's only Unseeli's metals that made our recent expansion possible. But Unseeli is the only place where these metals can be easily found, and we've become dependent on them. Without the regular supply ships these trees make possible, half our colonies would starve or suffocate or fall apart from lack of some essential. Millions would die, the Empire would collapse, and humanity would fall back into barbarism inside a generation.'

'To the Ashrai, we are barbarians,' said Carrion.

Silence shook his head impatiently. 'None of that matters any more. It's past. I need your help, Sean. Something's happened at Base Thirteen.'

Carrion looked at him steadily. 'The last time we met I called the Ashrai to arms and led them against the Empire. I led them into battle for the sake of their world, and you butchered them. You killed and slaughtered until you grew bored, and then you retreated into orbit and burned everything that lived.'

Silence didn't look away. 'It was necessary.'

'The Ashrai . . .'

'Didn't stand a chance. Rebels never do.'

'And you expect me to help you now? After everything that's happened, you expect me to help the Empire?'

'I could get you Pardoned.'

'I doubt that.'

Silence smiled coldly. 'Don't flatter yourself, Sean. You're not that important, or a bounty hunter would have taken your head years ago. No; you're just another deserter who went native on some backwater planet. No one cares about you any more. I can get you Pardoned, and I can take you off planet. Take you anywhere you want to go. You could start again; start over with a clean record. Think about it. You wouldn't even have to call yourself Carrion any more.'

'Why not, Captain? It's who I am.' Carrion shook his head slowly, and sank back in his chair. 'Thank you for the offer, Captain, but no.'

'No? Think what I'm offering you! You can't want to stay here on your own . . .'

'Can't I? I've found peace here.'

'What peace? The peace of the dead, of the cemetery?'

'The peace of the forest, Captain. You never did

understand what you were destroying. The Ashrai and the trees were linked more closely than you ever knew. The trees are alive. I've seen branches sway when no wind blows, and heard voices on the wind and in the mists. The Ashrai are dead, but they are not gone. There's a harmony, a strength that holds the trees together, and I'm a part of it.' The outlaw's voice fell to a whisper, his gaze still fixed on Silence's. 'Leave me alone, John. Please.'

'I can't, Sean. I need you.'

'Why, Captain? Why does it always have to be me?'

'Because you're the best.'

'Thank you, Captain.'

Silence turned away from the bitterness in Carrion's voice, and rose to his feet. 'Up you get, Carrion. It's a long way back to Base Thirteen, and we've a lot to discuss on the way.'

Carrion looked up at him. 'Are you so sure I'll help you?'

'Of course. You were my friend. And it's not as if you have anything else to do, is it?'

CHAPTER FIVE

Ghost in the Machine

The esper Diana Vertue leaned back in her seat and glared moodily at the pinnace monitors. The AI was still trying to make some sense out of the garbled responses it was getting from inside Base Thirteen, but as far as she could see, it was getting nowhere fast. Diana supposed it was an encouraging sign that they were getting any kind of response, but it was looking more and more to her that what they were getting were just random responses from a damaged computer. She had suggested as much to Odin, but the AI ignored her. She was only an esper, and therefore the AI didn't have to listen to her if it didn't want to. Even an Artificial Intelligence rated higher than an esper.

Diana sighed, and stretched out her legs as best she could in the cramped confines of the cabin. She'd expected many things of her first official mission on an alien world, but boredom wasn't one of them. She'd almost reached the point where she would have welcomed the two marines back on board, just to have someone to talk to. At least they had something to do, even if it was only keeping a lookout and second-guessing the Security system. All she had to do was sit and watch the computer talking to itself, and wait for something to go wrong. Not that there was a whole lot she could do if it did. She sighed again, heavily, and indulged herself in a pout. It wasn't fair. She'd been allowed to do nothing ever since they'd touched down on this miserable planet. She'd pretty much reached the point where she would gladly have accepted anything new happening, up to and including a major catastrophe, just so long as she got to see a little action. Anything would be better than this.

Well, almost anything. She hadn't forgotten what had happened the last time she'd opened up her esp, on the way down. There *was* something here on Unseeli with them, and to hell with what the sensors said. And whatever it was, it was dangerous. She'd sensed a rage and a force beyond anything she'd ever encountered before, something so powerful it almost burned out her mind just looking at it. She'd kept her esp damped down low ever since, and had no intention of raising it again, no matter how bored she got. She frowned slightly, unhappy at the direction her thoughts were taking, but unable to ignore them either. Captain Silence had known what her attackers were, even if what he'd said had made no sense. When he got back, she'd get some answers out of him; one way or another. She could always run a quick scan on him. In and out, so fast he'd never notice. But of course she couldn't. Just thinking about it was enough to make her stomach roll and sweat start on her face. The Empire conditioned its espers very carefully from childhood onwards, to ensure they'd never abuse their abilities. Except in the service of the Empire, of course.

'Investigator Frost to pinnace. Acknowledge, and confirm your situation.'

Diana sat up straight as the Investigator's cold, calm voice sounded in her comm implant. 'This is esper Vertue. The pinnace is still secure. Nothing's happened since you left. Where are you?'

'About two miles east from the landing field, map reference Alpha Tango eighty-eight. Has the Captain returned yet?'

'No, Investigator. He hasn't contacted us, and we haven't been able to raise him. Something down here is affecting the comm system; it only works when it feels like it.'

'I had hoped the Captain would be there, but we can proceed without him. This is an official Log Entry; Unseeli, fifteen forty-three hours. I have discovered what appears to be an alien space vessel, crashed some two miles east of Base Thirteen. The ship has suffered extensive damage, and there is as yet no sign of any pilot or other crew.'

'An alien ship?' said Diana excitedly as Frost paused. 'What type is it? What species?'

There was another pause, but when Frost spoke again, her voice was calm and measured. 'Unknown, esper.'

Diana stared blankly at the comm panels, her mind racing. Space-travelling aliens were rare, even out here on the Rim; but a new, unknown species ... This was the kind of thing careers were made on. A sudden thought struck her.

'Investigator; could this be a representative of the species who originally created the metal forest?'

'Possible, but unlikely. Any species intelligent enough to genegineer the trees would surely be able to land a ship without crashing it. Listen carefully, esper. You're going to have to leave the pinnace. I need you here, with me, to examine this ship. The marines will accompany you, to ensure your safety.'

'You mean; leave the pinnace unguarded?' said Diana.

'The pinnace can look after itself. Odin; go to full battle readiness. Acknowledge.'

'Acknowledged, Investigator.' The AI's voice was as calm and even as ever, but Diana would have sworn she heard something like excitement in its measured tones.

'In the meantime, Odin; keep trying to raise the Captain,' said Frost. 'I don't like being out of contact with him for so long. That goes for you too, esper. You might have better luck once you've moved away from the vicinity of Base Thirteen. Odin; what's your current status on repairs?'

'Progressing well, Investigator. All main systems are back on line and operational again.'

'What about structure integrity? Could we lift off again, if we had to?'

'Unknown, Investigator. Theoretically, yes. In practice, I could not recommend it, except in the direst of circumstances.'

'Very well. Maintain regular contact with the *Darkwind* after the esper and the marines have left; keep them up to date on what's happening down here. And be prepared to relay information from me to the *Darkwind*. I'll want the data from this new ship compared with existing records.'

'I'm afraid that won't be possible, Investigator. I have been unable to contact the *Darkwind* from the moment we landed. There is nothing wrong with the comm systems, so I can only conclude it is either a result of natural conditions, or the interference is deliberate.'

'What do you mean, we're out of contact?' snapped Frost. 'Why didn't you say anything before?'

'You didn't ask.'

'Computer; once this mission is over, you and I are going to have a long chat about which of us is in charge here. In the meantime, you will report to me, or the esper, or anybody else available, on any change in our circumstances that might affect our mission, *as they happen.* And if I have any further problems with you, I will personally reprogram your data banks with a shrapnel grenade. Is that clear?'

'There is no need to raise your voice to me, Investigator. I assure you, I have only the best interests of this mission at heart. I exist only to serve.'

'Blow it out your terminal.'

Diana looked aghast at the comm panels before her. Being cut off from the main ship was serious; it not only meant they were denied the ship's superior computer facilities, it also meant they were on their own if anything went wrong. Diana hugged herself tightly. She'd never been cut off from the ship from the moment she joined its crew. She was used to its protection always being there, only a call away. Now she felt alone, naked. Defenceless. She realised Frost was still talking, and made herself pay attention.

'If something is blocking our transmissions, can you determine their position in relation to ours?'

'Not at present, Investigator,' said the AI. 'Without further evidence, it remains only a hypothesis.'

'That settles it. Esper; I want you with me as fast as you can travel. The sooner we check this alien ship out, the better. And esper; keep your eyes open on the way. Investigator out.'

The silence that followed Frost's signing off had a definite feeling of uncertainty. Not to mention unease. The presence of the alien ship could explain a lot of things, but for the moment it raised more

questions than it answered. And the thought of
leaving the pinnace and travelling through the metallic forest was not a comforting one, even with the
marines for protection. Diana got to her feet and then
stood there dithering, unsure what to do first. She'd
wanted a little action, a little excitement, but this was
ridiculous. A thought struck her, and she turned to
glare at the comm panels.

'Odin; why didn't your sensors detect the presence
of the crashed alien ship?'

'Unknown, esper. Either the ship is shielded in
some way, or it and its crew are simply too alien to
show up on my instruments.'

Diana frowned. 'I thought it was impossible for
anything to shield itself from your sensors?'

'Impossible for any technology I am aware of. The
alien ship's level of technology is unknown.'

Diana growled something under her breath, and
strode down the cabin to the airlock. Even when the
computer was talking to her, she couldn't get anything useful out of it. At least the Investigator understood her worth. Just let her at that alien ship; she'd
show them what an esper could do. She'd show them
all.

The marines accepted their new orders with hardly
any fuss. Secretly, Diana thought they were probably
just as bored as she'd been. The news of an alien ship
didn't throw them at all. They just nodded, checked

the power levels on their guns, and led her off the landing field and into the metallic forest. They walked on either side of her, studying the surrounding trees alertly, their disrupters drawn and ready for use. Diana looked at the guns, and scowled. There was always the chance the aliens weren't involved with whatever had happened at Base Thirteen, and were just innocent bystanders. The Empire's usual reaction to a new species was to shoot first and ask questions later, if at all, but Diana was determined that wasn't going to happen here. First contacts could be peaceful, and she was going to do everything in her power to see that this one was. The Empire wasn't going to add another servant species to its ranks, another people to treat and exploit as second-class citizens. Like the espers.

She didn't like the way her thoughts were going, so she concentrated instead on her surroundings. The metallic trees were very beautiful, shining in the mists like frozen fireworks. Now that she was seeing them up close, walking among them, they didn't seem nearly as imposing. Their warm glow seemed friendly, even inviting ... Which was more than she could say about the entities that had attacked her on the way down. The day seemed suddenly colder, and she shuddered quickly. She'd never felt a rage like it, an anger beyond thought or emotion; a force in itself. A force strong enough to break through a pinnace hull built to withstand atomics. She looked at the

marines walking with her, and her brief feeling of
security was gone, as though it had never been. Guns
and cold steel would be little use against the kind of
force she'd sensed.

She thrust the thought out of her mind. She was on
her way to an unknown alien ship and a possible first
contact, and nothing was going to spoil that for her.
She wouldn't let anything spoil it. She lengthened her
stride, almost skipping along in her enthusiasm. The
marines had to hurry to keep up with her. Ripper
studied her thoughtfully, and Stasiak gave her a dark
look or two, but she ignored both of them. And then
the smile left her face and the joy went out of her in
a moment, as something moved in the trees, not far
away. She stopped dead in her tracks, and the marines
stopped with her. They looked at her enquiringly,
and she tried hard to stop trembling.

'Didn't you hear it?' she said quietly.

'Hear what?' said Stasiak, trying to look in every
direction at once, and almost succeeding.

'There's something moving in the mists, not far
away. It knows we're here.' She frowned, concentrating, trying to touch whatever it was with her esp, but
it stayed obstinately just at the edge of her awareness.

'Can you at least give us a direction?' said Ripper
quietly.

Diana indicated off to her right with a quick movement of her chin, and they all strained their eyes

against the mists. It was cold and quiet and nothing moved.

'There's nothing there,' said Stasiak, lowering his gun. 'Not a damned thing. You're just nervous, esper. Jumping at shadows.'

'It's there,' said Diana. 'I can feel it.'

'Well whatever it is, I think we'd be safer on the move,' said Ripper. 'Lou; you lead the way. I'll watch the rear. Esper; you stay between us, and if you see it again, try and let us know without alerting it. Don't worry; we won't let anything happen to you. Now let's move, shall we? Nice and easy . . .'

They set off again, and Diana strode jerkily along, looking left and right, her back crawling. Something was watching her, and she could feel its menace like a sharp taste in her mouth. Her hands clenched into fists at her sides, and she almost wished she had taken a disrupter for herself after all. The thought shocked her calm again, like a faceful of cold water. She was an esper, not a killer. Whatever it was out there, she should be concentrating on making contact with it. Only, there was no other living thing on this planet. The sensors said so. But the sensors hadn't reacted to her attackers on the way down, and they'd been real enough. She'd felt them in her mind as they moved in inexorably to crush the fragile pinnace, only to draw back when they sensed her presence. Her presence. *Because they knew you were innocent, the*

Captain had said. The word innocent rang in her mind
like a bell.

There was a loud crashing sound to her left, as
something large forced its way between two trees,
snapping off the solid metal branches as it did. Ripper
signalled urgently for them to keep moving. Diana
looked at Stasiak.

'Still think I'm seeing things?'

He growled something under his breath, swinging
his gun back and forth as he searched for a target.
There was the sound of heavy footsteps, to their left
and to their right, and the ground shook under their
feet. Diana's breath caught in her throat as she realised
the sounds were coming from two different directions now. She began to increase her pace, and the
marines moved with her, until suddenly all three of
them were running. The heavy footsteps kept up with
them effortlessly, the ground shaking under their
weight like an earthquake. Diana could feel panic
welling up inside her, and clamped down on it hard.
Whatever was out there, it wanted them to know
about it. She could feel herself slowing as her wind
ran out, and forced herself on. And then they burst
out of the trees and into a clearing, and as suddenly
as that the pursuing footsteps were gone. The three
of them stumbled to a halt, looking back into the
trees, but the mists were empty and still, the only
sound on the quiet their own harsh breathing.

'What happened?' said Stasiak breathlessly. 'Did we lose it?'

'I don't think so,' said Diana.

'Then what did happen?' said Ripper.

Diana shrugged. 'They're not ready to kill us yet, that's all. They want us to suffer first.'

'They?' said Ripper. 'Diana; who are *they*?'

The esper looked away from the trees and turned her gaze on the two marines. 'They're the Ashrai. Or what's left of them. Angry ghosts haunting the forest that used to be theirs.'

She began to breathe more easily again, and nodded for the two marines to continue. They glared at the trees around them, hefted their guns uncertainly, and then started across the open clearing. Diana moved with them, her esp wide open, but she couldn't detect any other presences in the surrounding forest. All three of them tensed as they left the clearing and plunged back into the trees, but nothing happened. They stayed alert and cautious all the rest of the way, but the forest remained empty and silent, like a huge abandoned graveyard. And finally they arrived at their destination, with nothing to show for their trip but a few jangled nerves. They stopped at the top of a rise and looked down at what they'd come to see, and for a long time none of them could say anything.

The crashed alien ship lay at the bottom of the rise, huge and dark like a thunder cloud fallen to earth. It was hundreds of feet long, an insane tangle of brass columns, held together by glazed nodes each bigger than the entire pinnace. Spiked and barbed projections emerged from the main bulk at irregular intervals, but whether they were sensors or weapons or something else entirely wasn't clear. The ship lay half buried at the end of a mile-long scorch mark, with a long trail of jagged tree stumps to mark its passing. Diana tried to imagine how fast the ship had to have been travelling when it hit, to have caused such devastation, but it was just too much for her to visualise. The one thing she was sure of was that the pinnace wouldn't have survived such a landing. She looked round sharply as someone called her name, and then she hurried down to join the Investigator waiting by the ship. The marines followed her down at a more leisurely pace, just to remind the Investigator that they weren't that impressed by her.

The ship loomed over Diana like a mountain crag, its dull brass surfaces seeming to absorb the light rather than reflect it. The Investigator ignored it casually, as though she'd seen better, in her time. *Probably has*, thought Diana.

'You're later than I expected,' said Frost. 'Trouble along the way?'

'Not really,' said Ripper easily. 'We thought we heard something moving in the mists, but nothing came of it.'

Frost nodded, apparently unconcerned. 'You

marines will stand watch while the esper and I check out the ship. Nothing is to approach this vessel without being challenged and identified first. But don't just blast anything that moves. Remember; the Captain's still out there somewhere. Esper; follow me.'

She turned and walked away, and Diana hurried after her. The alien ship fascinated her. Its shape made no sense at all, and trying to follow the ins and outs of its insane structure made her dizzy. The twisting brass columns ranged from two to twenty feet in diameter, wrapped around each other as often as not.

'It is an unknown, isn't it, Investigator?' she burst out finally, unable to keep quiet any longer. 'It's a totally new alien species! I've never seen anything like it.'

'Neither have I,' said Frost calmly. 'Run a full scan on it for me.'

Diana flushed. She shouldn't have needed an order to do something that basic. She raised her esp and let it flow out over the ship. The huge structure burned in her mind like a guttering candle, and she grimaced despite herself. She couldn't seem to get a hold on anything; her mind skidded off the ship as though it were greased. She concentrated, trying to focus, but the ship was so different, so ... alien, her mind simply couldn't grasp it. There was something deeply disturbing about the vessel, with all its crazy angles and weird surfaces, things that shouldn't hold together but somehow did, and above it all ... something else. Something so large, so enormous she couldn't see it for the details. She pulled back, trying to grasp the whole structure as one, and when the truth finally hit her she couldn't get her breath for a moment.

Frost studied the esper as she stood before the ship, her eyes moving restlessly behind her closed eyelids. Diana's breathing was quick and shallow, and there was a sheen of sweat on her face despite the cold. And then the esper's eyes shot open, and she fell back a step, her hands lifting as though to defend herself from something close at hand. She looked away from the ship, shuddered quickly, and then had herself back under control again. Frost frowned. Whatever the esper had encountered, it was apparently unpleasant enough to knock all the enthusiasm for the ship right out of her.

'Well?' said Frost finally. 'What did you see, esper?'

'I'm not sure,' said Diana quietly. 'The ship is so alien I can't be sure of anything.'

'Did you detect any life signs within the ship?'

'Just one.' Diana looked at the Investigator for the first time. 'I think it's the ship itself. And it's dying.'

Frost looked at the unhappy esper for a moment, and then nodded and turned away. She studied the vast wreck towering over her, and walked slowly along beside it. Diana hurried after her, not wanting to be left alone, even for a moment.

Up on the rise, Stasiak looked at Ripper. 'Do you get the feeling we're ever so slightly superfluous here?'

Ripper shrugged. 'There's always the chance those ghosts will show up to annoy us again.'

'Oh great. What are we supposed to do; exorcise them? I'm getting really fed up with this mission, Rip. Nothing to hit, nothing to shoot at, and I think my suit's heating elements are on the blink again.'

'Look on the bright side,' said Ripper. 'At least it's not raining.'

Stasiak just stared at him.

Frost stood before the huge alien ship, and let her hand rest on the butt of her gun. If she didn't find an entrance soon, she'd make one the hard way. She didn't like resorting to brute force so early in an investigation, but this whole mission had been a debacle right from the beginning. Standard procedure with any new species was to study the situation from a safe distance, and only make contact when you were sure you held the upper hand. But here she was, thrown in the deep end and sinking fast, with the Captain off on his own somewhere looking for ghosts, and no back-up from the main ship if things looked like getting out of hand. Frost sighed, and shook her head. Some days you just shouldn't get out of bed in the morning.

She scowled at the ship, and gently reached out to touch the dully gleaming metal with her fingertips. It was surprisingly warm, with an unpleasant oily feel.

'Investigator!'

Frost looked away from the hull, absently rubbing her fingers together. 'What is it, esper?'

'I've found something. It could be a hatchway.'

Frost looked back and winced inwardly as she saw the esper had climbed on to a metal turret, and was squatting precariously before a shadowy niche. Frost pondered briefly if there was any point in raising the subject of security systems and booby traps, and decided not to waste her breath. With the esper's luck they'd probably just malfunction anyway. She climbed carefully up to join Diana, her hands and feet slipping on the slick metal, and looked at what the esper had found. Tucked away behind a metal out-cropping was a dark gap, some ten feet tall and three feet wide.

'It's not an air lock,' said the esper excitedly. 'But the shape's too regular for it to be crash damage. Do we go in?'

Frost frowned. 'Normally, I'd say no. We don't know enough about the ship to tell what's dangerous and what isn't. But, since we're pressed for time and we need answers now, yes, esper; we are going in. Or rather, I'm going in and you're coming along to watch my back. Stay close, but don't get in my way. Odin; this is Investigator Frost. Respond.'

They waited for a moment but there was no reply, not even static from their comm implants. Frost gestured for Diana to try her comm unit, but she did no better.

'Damn,' said Frost dispassionately. 'Something in the ship must be interfering with our transmissions. This mission just gets better all the time. Follow me, esper.'

Frost drew her disrupter and stepped cautiously through the opening. Diana followed her in, practically treading on the Investigator's heels. Beyond the opening lay a narrow tunnel choked with thick strands of filmy webbing, some of which was already falling apart in shreds and tatters. The ceiling was too low for the esper and the Investigator to walk upright, and they were forced to proceed in a hunched, awkward shuffle. A flickering blue light emanated from the corridor walls, hiding as much in shadows as it revealed. The air was definitely warmer inside the ship, and Diana wrinkled her nose at the growing sickly sweet smell. It reminded her of something, but she couldn't place it. She tried instead to concentrate on what the corridor was telling her about the ship's inhabitants. To start with, they were definitely shorter than humans, probably about four feet or less in height. The blue lights suggested eyes that functioned in roughly the same range as a human's, and the warmer air suggested a need for temperature controls.

Beyond that, Diana was pretty much out of her depth, and she knew it.

Frost holstered her gun, drew her sword and began methodically cutting a path through the decaying webbing. The strands gave way easily enough, but there was little room to swing the great sword in the confines of the corridor, and the Investigator's progress was slowed by a need to stop every now and again to clean away threads clinging stubbornly to the blade. The light grew steadily brighter as they slowly made their way deeper into the ship, but the flickering grew worse, if anything. Diana shrugged mentally. Maybe the light was supposed to flicker.

The smell was stronger. The uneven floor rose and fell like a tide, and the walls bowed in and out for no reason Diana could see. Faint silver traces shone along one wall, though whether they were functional or merely decorative was unclear. Certainly the patterns followed no human sense of logic or aesthetics. Openings appeared in the walls, leading off into other corridors, some of which were unlit. Diana began to be a little nervous about how far they'd come, and glanced back over her shoulder. The tunnel stretched away into the blue-lit distance, with no sign of the entrance they'd used. Diana decided she wasn't going to think about that. No doubt Frost knew the way out, and that was all that mattered. In the meantime, there were just too many interesting things to get excited about.

'Isn't this amazing?' she said breathlessly to the Investigator as she paused yet again to clean her sword.

Frost smiled slightly, but didn't answer. The esper might be wide-eyed with the wonder of it all, but Frost knew better than to let herself get distracted. There'd be time for sightseeing later, when the ship had been thoroughly explored and tested for booby traps, intentional and otherwise. She pressed on cautiously, carefully checking each side passage before they passed it. The ship was eerily quiet, the hush seeming almost to absorb each new sound as it was made. And there was a growing feeling on the air, something clinging, like static. Frost suddenly realised the esper wasn't treading on her heels any more, and she looked back down the corridor. Diana had come to a halt some way back, and was staring intently at the ceiling above her. Frost padded quietly back to join her.

'What is it, esper? What have you found?'

'I'm not sure,' said Diana slowly. 'Look at this.'

She gestured at part of the ceiling. It was blue and purple and swollen, like a bruise. Frost tested it with the tip of her sword, and the material gave easily under the pressure.

'I finally recognised the smell,' said Diana. 'It's a lot clearer just here.'

Frost looked at her dubiously and took a deep breath, flaring her nostrils. Together with the look of the ceiling, the sickly sweet smell was immediately familiar. 'Decay,' said Frost. 'Rotting meat.'

'Yes,' said Diana. 'Decomposition of what was once living tissue. Parts of the ship have been dead long enough to rot.'

Frost hefted her sword, took a firm grip with both hands, and cut savagely at the discoloured patch on the ceiling. The blade sank in deep, the bruised-looking material splitting open like a wound. Frost jerked her sword back out, and tangled silver threads fell down into the corridor, wrapped around pink ropes of intestines, studded with faceted crystals. Diana fell back a step, a look of almost comical surprise on her face. Frost touched a cautious finger to the hanging threads, and they fell apart into a gooey slime that spattered on the floor. Frost studied it for a moment, and then wiped her fingers clean on her leggings. She couldn't perform a proper analysis without her equipment, and most of that was stuck back on the Darkwind. She blinked in surprise as the esper fell suddenly to her knees beside the slime on the floor, and gently parted it with her fingers. Frost knelt down beside her, and Diana fished a small faceted crystal out of the goo, and held it up before her eyes.

'What is it?' said Frost.

'It's a memory crystal,' said Diana. 'Pretty much like the ones we use in our computers. Only here the patterns are so strongly impressed I can practically read them with my mind. I could be wrong, but I think this is part of this ship's log.' She got to her feet along with the Investigator, still holding the crystal up before her eyes. 'The other crystals are either dead or damaged; I'm not getting anything from them. But this one . . . this crystal is important. I can feel it.'

Frost nodded slowly, swinging her sword thoughtfully back and forth before her. 'Take it back to the pinnace, and let Odin have a crack at it. I want a complete analysis, and access to the crystal's memories, and I want it an hour ago. So you'd better hurry.'

Diana looked at her blankly. 'You mean; we're leaving? But we've barely scratched the surface here!'

'You're leaving. I'm staying. I think we can be fairly sure there aren't any living crew left on board, or you'd have sensed them by now. So the only answers we're likely to get are from that crystal. Take the marines back with you; the crystal needs their protection more than I do. Well don't just stand there, esper; what are you waiting for?'

'I can't find my way back out on my own,' said Diana in a small voice. 'Can you come back with me to show me the way?'

Stasiak looked at Ripper, and then back at Diana. 'Leave her here? Are you sure?'

'That's what she said,' said Diana. 'Do you want to argue with her?'

'Not really, no,' said Ripper.

'I don't know, Rip,' said Stasiak. 'Anything could happen in there.'

'Anyone else and I might be worried,' said Ripper. 'But we are talking about an Investigator, after all. Anything that runs into her has my deepest sympathies. Besides, do you really want to look her in the eye later and tell her you ignored a direct order?'

'Not particularly, no.' Stasiak looked down the slope at the ship below. 'What's it like in there, Diana?'

'Fascinating!' Now that she was out of the ship and back in the open again, Diana lost her nervousness and found herself bubbling with excitement, almost ready to rush back into the ship and explore it again. Almost. 'I've never seen anything like it; the whole structure's a combination of organic and inorganic materials, lying side by side and functioning together.'

'You mean, like a cyborg?' said Stasiak, peering uncertainly at the huge shape below them.

'I suppose so, yes, but on a much vaster scale. The entire thing's alive, or at least it used to be. I'd love to spend more time with it, but the Investigator was most insistent we get this memory crystal back to the pinnace. Typical. The moment you find anything interesting, the Empire immediately finds a way to take it away from you.'

Stasiak smiled. 'If you can't take a joke, you shouldn't have joined.'

'I wasn't exactly given a choice,' said Diana. 'Espers do what they're told.'

And then the wry smile vanished from her face as she looked past Stasiak. The two marines spun round to discover what she was looking at, and their hands fell to their guns. Among the violet and azure trees at the edge of the forest, a man dressed all in black was walking unhurriedly out of the mists. His face was hidden by his cape's cowl, but they all knew who he was, who he had to be. He walked past them without sparing any of them a glance, and started down the slope towards the alien ship. Diana shuddered despite herself as he passed, and had to fight down a sudden urge to reach out and touch him, to make sure he was real, even though the sensors said he wasn't. Instead, she watched silently with the marines as the man in black came to a halt before the ship, and looked at it thoughtfully, leaning elegantly on his ivory staff.

'Is that him?' said Diana softly. 'I thought he'd be taller.'

'Not very impressive,' said Ripper. 'But then, legends rarely are, in the flesh.'

'Carrion,' said Stasiak, his voice low and harsh. 'The man who lived with the Ashrai. The traitor who turned against humanity, for the sake of savages who still ate their meat raw. I've done some things in my time, and been ashamed of some of them, but I never betrayed my own species. Never.'

'Take it easy, Lou,' said Ripper. 'We don't know the whole story.'

'We don't need to.'

'Why does the Captain think he's so important?' said Diana. 'I mean, all right, he can fool the pinnace's sensors, but he's just another outlaw. Isn't he?'

'Carrion's a killer,' said Captain Silence. 'And he's very good at it.'

The esper and the two marines spun round again, to see Silence standing at the edge of the forest behind them, leaning against a tree trunk for support.

'Captain!' said Diana, blushing in spite of herself. 'I didn't hear you approach . . .'

'Obviously,' said Silence. 'Security on this mission is going to hell.' He broke off, grimacing as pain from his injured ribs hit him. Diana took in his torn and blood-stained uniform and started towards him, but he stopped her with an upraised hand. 'I'm all right. I just ran into a little opposition from the local ghosts. Carrion rescued me. And no, I don't want to talk about it. Odin told me about the Investigator's discovery, after he'd finished filling me in on all the security lapses first, of course, and I brought Carrion along to take a look at it. How long have you been here?'

'Not long,' said Diana. 'The Investigator and I made a brief foray into the ship, but there's no sign of any crew. We did find what appears to be an alien memory crystal. The Investigator decided it should go back to the pinnace for analysis. She's still inside the ship.'

'I thought she might be,' said Silence. 'Carrion's going to join her. Between them, they should come up with some answers.'

'Pardon me for asking, Captain,' said Stasiak, 'but what makes the traitor so important?'

'Carrion used to be an Investigator,' said Silence. 'One of the best. Trained to out-think species that don't think as we do.'

'If he was that good,' said Ripper, 'what went wrong? How did he end up siding with the Ashrai?'

Silence smiled humourlessly. 'Perhaps we trained him too well.'

He looked down at the alien ship below, and the others followed his gaze. Carrion had climbed on to the ship, and was examining the entrance Diana had found. His black cloak hung about him like folded wings, and he looked more than ever like a carrion crow, feasting on a dead carcass.

'What's that staff he's carrying?' said Stasiak.

'A power lance,' said Silence.

'But they're outlawed!'

Silence smiled briefly. 'So's he.'

Carrion threaded his way through the twisting, intertwining corridors of the alien ship, following the ragged path Frost had cut through the webbing. It led him eventually to a vast circular chamber deep in the heart of the ship, a great metal cavern studded with bulky, enigmatic machinery on all sides. The curving walls were pockmarked with tunnel mouths of various sizes, many high above the floor with no obvious way of reaching them. Thick strands of rotting gossamer hung from the ceiling, interspersed with long crystalline creepers that gleamed and sparkled in the unsteady light as they turned slowly back and forth. The flickering light came from deep in the tunnels, casting strange elongated shadows on the floor and ceiling. The air was hot and humid and thick with the stench of rotting meat. Frost stepped out of the shadows and into the light, and Carrion nodded to her courteously.

'I know you,' said Frost.

'No,' said Carrion. 'That was someone else. I am Carrion. I bring bad luck. I am the destroyer of nations and of worlds.'

Frost raised an eyebrow. 'Really?'

'The Ashrai believed it.'

They studied each other for a while in the uncertain light, and whatever they recognised in each other's faces they kept to themselves.

'I'm surprised you remember me,' said Carrion finally. 'It's been a long time.'

'All Investigators remember you,' said Frost. 'The Academy still holds you up as a bad example. You broke the prime rule; you got involved.'

'I broke my conditioning,' said Carrion. 'But then, I

was always involved, with one species or another. When you've spent half your life learning to move your mind in alien ways, it becomes hard to think in wholly human terms any more.'

Frost shrugged. 'Empathy's a useful tool, but that's all. Aliens are for killing. I've found something interesting. Come and take a look.'

She led him into a small compartment off the main chamber, through an opening so low they had to crawl through on hands and knees. The compartment was filled with spiky machinery that flowed seamlessly into the walls and floor. The ceiling was just high enough to let them stand upright, and suffused everything with a dull red glow that was disturbingly organic. The floor was uneven, solid ridges rising like bones to press against their boots in undulating rhythms. Everywhere, high-tech instruments blended into organic constructs, living and unliving components functioning side by side, as though the ship had been grown as much as made.

'This appears to be the control centre,' said Frost. 'Or one of them, anyway. I've traced a whole series of power lines that converge here, but I can't be sure until I can get some of my equipment down from the Darkwind.'

'Have you identified the main power source?'

Frost shook her head angrily. 'I can't even find the hyperdrive. By any reasonable standards this thing shouldn't even fly, let alone jump across the stars.'

Carrion nodded, his eyes vague and far away. 'Perhaps I can find the drive for you.'

A breeze from nowhere ruffled his cloak, and Frost's hackles rose as strange lights glowed suddenly in the instruments around them. There was a feeling of pressure on the air, of something unstoppable. A hatch shot open in the wall beside her, and slammed shut again like metal jaws. Instruments extended and reshaped themselves in subtle ways, and far off in the distance Frost thought she could hear something howling in anger and agony, as though the decaying ship had been somehow stirred to horrid life again. Carrion was smiling, and it was not a pleasant smile, his dark eyes fixed on something only he could see. Frost's hand drifted casually closer to the holstered gun at her side. At that moment, the outlaw seemed every bit as alien and as dangerous as the ship they were investigating. A loud juddering sound vibrated through the floor, rattling their teeth and shaking their heads, and then the floor opened up in the centre and a great tower of steel and diamond rose up into the chamber, shining so brightly they had to turn their heads away. Deep in the tunnels the howling died away, and a sudden silence filled the chamber as the alien machinery grew still. Carrion and Frost slowly turned back to look at the tower, shielding their eyes with their arms.

'I didn't know you were a polter,' said Frost.

'I would have thought it'd be in my file.'

'Your file's *Restricted*.'

'It would be,' said Carrion.

They peered more closely at the structure before them, as their eyes adjusted to the glare. The tower was an intricate latticework of metals, complex and mysterious, surrounding a brilliant cluster of glowing crystals. There was meaning and purpose in its structure, but none of it human.

'What is it?' whispered Frost, impressed despite herself.

Carrion smiled slowly. 'Judging by the remaining power flow, this is the ship's hyperdrive. Even if it does look nothing like ours. The Empire uses crystal technology in its computers; apparently these aliens found other uses for it.'

CHAPTER SIX

Inside Base Thirteen

The esper Diana Vertue sat slumped in her seat in the pinnace, and wondered why she still didn't feel safe. It had come on her suddenly, as they were walking back through the metallic forest to the landing field. Without any specific cause that she could name, Diana had suddenly been convinced that they were being watched, by something huge and awful and dangerous. Her stomach lurched. She managed to keep from crying out, but the feeling of imminent danger persisted, even though she couldn't see or hear anything to justify it. Nothing moved in the mists among the trees, and the only sounds were the quiet voices and footsteps of the people with her. Diana raised her esp and threw it out, scanning for anything near or approaching the group. Nothing had changed. The trees blazed in her mind like exclamation points of light, but there was no trace of any other living thing in the forest. She cast her net wider, till her mind fell over Base Thirteen, and she saw something looking back at her.

It was huge and dark, filling the Base, and it looked

at her with hungry eyes. There were voices screaming in the background, human voices, full of anguish and horror. There was a blood-red feeling of menace, of danger close and deadly, and then it was all gone, as suddenly as if she'd imagined it. She focused her esp on the Base, but there was nothing there now. If there ever had been.

She hadn't told the others what she'd sensed. She had no proof, and it had all happened so fast she wasn't sure she trusted it herself. It had the hot, hazy feeling of a fever dream, its very vagueness part of what was so horrifying. So she stayed silent, all the way back to the pinnace, and once she was aboard she curled up in her seat like a dog in its box, and tried to put it out of her mind. Only that was somehow worse, so she instructed the AI to patch in an exterior view through her comm implant. The steel bulkheads seemed to become transparent as the computer broadcast a real-time view of what its sensors were picking up. There was nothing but the landing pads and the trees and the swirling mists, the two marines standing guard, and the Base, waiting inside its impenetrable Screen. She should have felt safe and secure, protected by the pinnace and its weaponry, but somehow she only felt more visible, more vulnerable. The pinnace was the only ship on the pads, seeming a small and obvious target against the size of the landing field and the endless forest that surrounded it. She kept a careful watch in every direction, unable to settle but unwilling to raise her esp again for fear of drawing the watcher's attention back to her.

The more she put off telling anyone, the more it seemed to her nothing but an attack of nerves, a product of her own fear and insecurity. She tried to recapture some of the enthusiasm she'd felt about contacting the new alien species from the crashed ship, and that helped her push back the fear a little. It was just nerves, exacerbated by the waiting and the tension. She'd be all right, when the time finally came to enter the Base. But in the meantime she kept her eyes open and her mind damped right down, just in case.

The marines had felt something of it too. They'd been jumpy all the way back to the pinnace, and had seemed almost relieved when Silence ordered them to stand guard outside the ship. Silence, on the other hand, seemed strangely calm and relaxed, despite the beating he'd taken on his way to meet Carrion. He still wouldn't talk about that. He sat stoically as the ship's med unit stuck him with half a dozen needles, and then adjusted his uniform so that it provided more support for his ribs. And now he sat comfortably in his seat, half reclining, talking calmly with the AI about the memory crystal Diana had found in the alien ship. Odin had swallowed the crystal some time back, but apparently was having to create a whole new series of diagnostics just to access the damned thing. Diana smiled briefly. If she'd known it was going to be this much trouble, she'd have used her esp on the crystal and accessed the memories directly. Only that would have meant raising her esp again, and she wasn't ready to do that, not just yet.

Silence scowled at the comm panels before him. Given time, the AI could make the crystal do everything but sit up and beg, but they didn't have that much time. The Empire wanted the mining machinery working again, and it wanted it now. If he couldn't deliver, they'd send someone else to replace him. And that really would be the end of his career. Silence sighed slowly, careful of his ribs. The alien ship held the answer to what had happened in Base Thirteen, he was sure of it. One or more of the aliens had entered the Base, there'd been a conflict of some kind, and the Screen had gone up. Simple as that. But just in case it wasn't, he wanted the information in the alien memory crystal before he tried to break into the Base. Going into a potentially dangerous situation without a thorough briefing beforehand was never wise, and that went doubly here. With ghosts on the one hand and strange new aliens on the other, this had all the makings of a really messy disaster.

'Captain,' said a quiet voice behind him, 'I need to talk to you.'

'Not just now, esper, I'm busy.'

'You're supposed to be resting.'

'I'll rest later, when I've got time. I'm just waiting

for Carrion and Frost to return, and then we're going into Base Thirteen to scare up some answers.'

'Captain . . . if there are aliens inside the Base, we shouldn't be going in aggressively, looking for trouble. We should at least try to make contact with them. They could be peaceful. This could all be the result of some ghastly mistake or misunderstanding.'

Silence turned round in his seat and looked patiently at the young esper. 'This is all new to you, Diana, but the Empire has a set procedure when it comes to handling first contacts. And the first and main part of that procedure is that the Investigator will decide how we handle it. She's the expert.'

'An expert at killing.'

'Yes. The Empire doesn't like the idea of competition, so its attitude to aliens is really quite straightforward. They're either friendly, in which case they become part of the Empire, whether they want to or not, or they're unfriendly, in which case they get stepped on. Hard.'

'Like the Ashrai?' said Diana.

'Yes, esper. Like the Ashrai. I knew where my responsibilities lay, even then. Look, if I can see a way to sort this out without bloodshed, I'll take it. I don't believe in putting my people at risk unnecessarily. But I can't be optimistic about this. The most likely scenario is that one or more of the aliens have entered the Base and killed all the personnel.'

'You can't know that.'

'That's right, I can't. But that's how I have to play it. If whatever is in there is willing to talk, I'll listen, but they've made no move to contact us so far. Have you been able to pick up anything?'

'Just . . . impressions. Nothing I can be sure of. My own fears could be misinterpreting the little I am getting. Couldn't we at least wait till the AI's cracked the memory crystal? It could hold all the answers we need.'

'Esper, I don't even know if Odin can access it at all. We're dealing with an unknown technology here. The AI's good, but he can't work miracles. And I am running out of time and patience. I'll wait for Carrion and Frost to get back here, but then we have to go, ready or not.'

The esper's jaw muscles worked for a moment, but when she spoke her voice was calm and measured. 'I'd like to try something, Captain. I want permission to go into the Base on my own, once you've got us through the Screen, and attempt to make contact with my esp. They might not see one person as a threat.'

'My orders are quite specific,' said Silence. 'I'm to discover what happened inside Base Thirteen, and take whatever action is necessary to re-establish the Base and restore mining operations. Everything else is of secondary importance. There were one hundred and twenty-seven men and women in that Base. We've heard nothing from them since the Screen went up. The odds are, they're all dead. If they are, then whatever killed them has to die. The Empire can't afford to be seen to be weak.'

'Please, Captain. Listen to me.' Diana hesitated, torn between her need to explain what she was feeling, and the knowledge that she couldn't prove any of it. 'There's more to this than whatever came out of the crashed ship. I've felt things, on my way down in the pinnace, and later on . . . there's something incredibly powerful on this planet, Captain, and I don't think it's the aliens.'

'You're right,' said Silence. 'It's the Ashrai.'

Diana chose her words carefully. 'But they're all dead, Captain. You saw to that.'

'They may be dead,' said Silence, 'but they sleep lightly.'

'I could still use my esp to contact the aliens,' said Diana doggedly.

'No,' said Silence. 'The situation's complicated enough as it is.'

'So you'll leave it to the Investigator? The killer?'

'You say that as though it's an insult. She'd see it as a compliment. Investigators are the end result of the Empire's search for the perfect warrior. They started out working with the augmented men, the Wampyr and the Wolflings. That got out of hand with Haden, and the cyborg rebellion. So instead they created a breed of warrior that wasn't reliant on tech implants; a race of killers trained from childhood to be the best at everything. Strong, fast, intelligent, ruthless. And trained, most of all, to out-think things that don't think as we do. Frost is in charge of all alien contacts, and she will make whatever decisions are necessary. She's the expert. If you have anything further to say, take it up with her.'

'Would she listen, if I did?'

'I don't know. Maybe. She understands the value of an esper.'

'Perhaps I should talk to Carrion. He used to be an Investigator too, didn't he?'

'Yes,' said Silence. 'Yes, he did.'

Diana could feel his pain even with her shields up, and she had to look away for a moment. Through the transparent bulkhead she saw Carrion and Frost walk out of the mists and head towards the two marines, who apparently hadn't heard them coming, and were a bit upset about it. Silence followed her gaze, saw Carrion and looked away.

'You knew Carrion from before,' said Diana. 'What was he like, before he was a traitor?'

'He was my friend,' said Silence, and then he turned and left the cabin. Diana stood where she was, to give him a chance to get away, and then she followed him out.

Outside the pinnace, they all stood and looked at each other, as though waiting for someone else to start. Finally Silence nodded curtly to Carrion and

Frost. They were standing close together, and they stood in the same pose and moved in the same ways, like brother and sister. As though they had more in common with each other than they could ever have with anyone else. Silence knew he'd have to keep an eye on that. He couldn't risk losing Frost the way he'd lost Carrion.

'Any trace of the alien crew?' he said eventually.

'None,' said Frost. 'And their ship's dead. It's an interesting ship. The technology's like nothing I've ever seen before.'

Silence looked at Carrion. 'Could the crew have fled into the forest?'

'No, Captain. I'd have known.'

'And that just leaves the Base,' said Ripper. 'Surprise, surprise.'

'Tell me about the ship's technology,' said Silence. 'You said something earlier about a new kind of hyperdrive.'

'There was extensive use of living tissue alongside mechanical,' said Frost. 'Essentially, the ship was one great cybernetic unit, incredibly complex. And if the hyperdrive is what we think it is, it's far beyond anything the Empire has.'

There was a tense pause, as though they all had something to say, but no one wanted to be the first to say it. There were certain things it was wise never to say aloud, particularly when an Empire AI was listening. Their loyalty was programmed into them, and they tended to have very strict ideas about what constituted treason, or a threat to the Empire's security. Silence looked thoughtfully at Carrion.

'The aliens must be inside the Base.'

'Agreed, Captain.'

'And you're going to get us through the Screen.'

'No, Captain.'

Silence looked at him, and tension all but crackled on the air between them. The two marines let their hands move slightly so that they were both covering the traitor with their guns.

'I can break through the Screen,' said Carrion, 'but you're in no condition to enter the Base.'

'I'd have to agree,' said Frost. 'A Captain has no business exposing himself to unnecessary risks. That's standard procedure.'

'There's nothing standard about this mission,' said Silence tightly. 'I'm in charge here, and I'll make whatever decisions have to be made. To do that I need to be there, on the spot, as and when conditions change. And I've a feeling they could change pretty damned fast once we get inside the Base. I'm fit enough, and that's all that matters. I'm sure the marines are more than capable of seeing that nothing happens to me.'

'Right,' growled Stasiak, looking pointedly at Carrion. The outlaw ignored him. He looked over at Base Thirteen, hidden behind its shimmering opalescent Screen, and if there was any expression in his face, none of them could read it.

'Let's go,' he said calmly. 'The sooner we begin, the sooner we'll be finished. And God have mercy on those who die here.'

He started off towards the Base and, after a moment, Silence and Frost followed him. The others brought up the rear. Stasiak looked at Ripper.

'Cheerful bastard, isn't he?'

'What did you expect?' said Ripper. 'He used to be an Investigator.'

They stood together before Base Thirteen, and the glowing pearly Screen stared back at them, mute and enigmatic. Silence studied it sourly. It was as though the Screen was mocking him. Anything could be happening behind that impenetrable field of energy. Anything at all. Anyone else would have had to suffer its smug indifference, but he had an ace up his sleeve. He had Carrion. Silence looked at the outlaw. He was still standing beside Frost, so close their shoulders touched. They looked as though they should always be together, connected by a shared past and secrets too terrible to share with anyone else. Silence felt oddly jealous. Carrion used to be his friend. But that was years ago, when they were different people, and Silence was honest enough to admit that he would only have felt uncomfortable if Carrion had chosen to stand with him.

The marines were standing off a little to one side, their guns in their hands, keeping an unobtrusive eye on Carrion. To their way of thinking, he was the biggest threat to the party at present, so they'd watch him till something better came along. Marines were great ones for sticking to the problem at hand, and letting officers worry about the future. The esper was ignoring them all and scowling at the Screen, as though she could force her esp past it to see what lay beyond. Unfortunately, she wasn't that powerful. That was why Silence needed Carrion.

He looked at the outlaw, and sighed quietly to himself. He couldn't put it off any longer. It was time for the moment of truth, and let the chips fall where they may. He activated his comm implant.

'Odin; you are now in control of the pinnace. You will follow our entry into the Base through our eyes, and keep a complete record of all that occurs. If we fail in our mission, and none of us survive, you will make every effort to return to the *Darkwind*, and see that the record is made available to our successors. Acknowledge.'

'Acknowledged, Captain. Good luck.'

Silence looked at Carrion. 'It's time. Do your stuff.'

The outlaw nodded, his gaze fixed on the Screen. He stepped forward and reached out a hand to touch the energy field. Fat sparks of static sputtered on the air, but there was no other response. Which was interesting. It should have killed him stone dead. It would have killed anyone else. Carrion pressed hard against the Screen, but it didn't give. He smiled slightly, as though he'd expected that, and stepped back. He lifted his power lance and pressed the end of it against the energy field. A faint corona circled the end of the staff where it touched the Screen. Carrion increased the pressure, and the Screen gave way before it. Carrion took hold of the staff with both hands, and walked slowly forward into the energy field. The force field whorled and rippled around him, bands of iridescent light breaking over him in waves. He stood deep in the field, and the Screen that could ward off disrupters and withstand atomics drew reluctantly back from the outlaw's presence. An opening grew around him, through which the dark, squat shape of Base Thirteen could be seen. Carrion looked back at the others, and there was something not entirely human in his eyes.

'Now,' said Carrion, and they all stepped forward as though he had them on a leash. Silence kept his head up, but his skin crawled in anticipation of the lethal energies running through the force Screen, held back only by the power of one man's mind. By someone perhaps no longer entirely human. Finally they were all through, and Carrion remained in the field. He looked unhurriedly about him, colours waterfalling down around him in vivid shades that burned the eye. And then he stepped forward, and the energy field closed behind him as though it had never opened. No one could get out, and no one could get in to help, without Carrion's assistance. They were trapped with whatever lay inside Base Thirteen, and the force Screen covered them all.

'How did you do that?' said Diana, something that might have been awe softening her voice.

'His power lance,' said Frost, when it became clear the outlaw wasn't going to answer. 'It amplifies and channels his psychokinesis. You can guess why the Empire banned them. But even so, even with a power lance, what he just did is supposed to be impossible. His esper abilities must be right off the scale. I'm surprised the Empire ever let him run around loose.'

'Before he came to Unseeli,' said Silence, 'he showed no sign of any esp at all. His time with the Ashrai changed that.'

'That's impossible,' said Frost flatly. 'Everyone's tested for psi; no one escapes.'

'Nothing's impossible, for the Ashrai,' said Carrion.

'Your attention, please,' said Odin, its voice murmuring through everyone's implants. 'Captain; I've finally been able to glean something useful from the Base's computers' records. I've managed to isolate the Base Commander's personal log. I really think you should view what I've found, before you proceed any further.'

'All right,' said Silence. 'Since nothing nasty has come running out of the Base to attack us, I think we can safely wait a few more moments before we go in.

Marines; stand guard. If anything moves, shoot it. Odin; run the relevant parts of the log for everyone except the marines, then run it for them. How much is there?'

'Not much, Captain. I've selected what appear to be the important moments.'

A brief burst of static filled Silence's eyes as the AI ran the log through its comm implant. The static cleared to show the Base Commander, sitting at his desk. Silence frowned. He knew the man. James Starblood had been at the Fleet Academy in the same year as him. Old family. Not much money, but well connected. They'd known each other well for a short time, but had never really been friends. Starblood had been a hard-working, efficient officer, and about as imaginative as a stone. Which probably explained what he was doing in a post like this. Unseeli was not a posting for the upwardly mobile. Silence's frown deepened. The Commander looked haggard and confused, and when Starblood finally spoke, his voice was rough and unsteady.

'To whoever finds this log; this is an Alpha Red emergency. An alien ship has crashlanded nearby. It doesn't answer any of our attempts to make contact. I sent a team to investigate the crash site. They never came back. That was three hours ago. Now people are disappearing inside the Base. Something's affecting the computers. Whole sectors don't answer. The life-support systems are breaking down. The lights are going out. It's getting cold. There's something in here with us but we can't find it.'

The scene changed. Starblood was sitting slumped in his chair. He was sweating, and his uniform was dishevelled. He passed a shaking hand across his mouth, and tried visibly to pull himself together. 'I can't raise anyone in the Base, and something's happened to our main comm system. I can't contact the Empire, or even broadcast a warning. My personal log seems secure, for the moment. I've locked myself in my quarters and barricaded the door. I can hear something moving in the corridor outside. It doesn't sound human. I'm trapped in here. Base Thirteen is lost to the Empire. There's only one option left to me; raising the Screen.'

He reached out of view for a moment, and then looked up again, his eyes seeming to pierce Silence. There was despair in the man's face, but something else too. Something that might have been dignity. 'The force Screen is now activated. Whatever's in here is trapped inside the Base. I can't risk letting it escape. The Empire must know of this new threat. The Screen can only be lowered from inside now, using my personal code. I know my duty.' He drew a disrupter from the holster on his hip, and clumsily checked the power level. 'Haven't had to use one of these things in years,' he grumbled quietly, and then turned the gun on himself, centring it carefully over his heart. He looked up one last time.

'Whoever finds this message; avenge us. Protect the Empire. I am James Starblood, Commander of Base Thirteen.'

Silence's vision cleared to show the world again. He wished he'd liked the man more.

'That's all there is, Captain,' said Odin quietly.

'A hundred and twenty-seven people,' said Diana. 'All dead.'

'You didn't really expect anything else, did you?' said Frost. Diana shrugged, and looked away. There was a pause as the marines watched the message.

'Well, that was interesting,' said Stasiak brightly. 'We're facing something powerful enough to wipe out a whole Base, and all we've got are a few hand guns and an outlaw esper. Why don't we all just shoot ourselves now, and get it over with?'

'He's got a point,' said Ripper.

'Shut up,' said Frost calmly, and the two marines were immediately quiet. 'You've nothing to worry about. You've got me.' She looked at Silence. 'You're in charge, Captain. What do we do?'

'We go in,' said Silence. 'And we do whatever's necessary.'

He walked towards the open front doors, with Carrion and Frost following close behind. The esper hurried to catch up. The marines shared a meaningful glance, and reluctantly brought up the rear. The Base itself looked calm and deserted. No lights were showing anywhere. The front doors were standing just a

little ajar. Silence stopped before them and studied
the steel doors carefully. There was a thick layering of
hoarfrost on the metal, and the doors hung limply
from their supports. Carrion reached out and pushed
one door, and it moved uneasily under his touch, all
power gone. He pushed it all the way open, and he
and Silence stepped forward into the gloom of the
Lobby.

Unseeli's cold had entered the Base, giving the stale
air a cutting edge. None of the lights were working,
and as far as Silence could see the Lobby was entirely
deserted. Carrion and Frost moved quickly in to stand
on either side of him, eyes searching the shadows for
an ambush. All was still and quiet; the only sound
their own breathing. Frost sniffed suspiciously, her
gun in her hand as though it belonged there. Carrion
leaned elegantly on his power lance, apparently
happy for Silence to take the initiative. The esper
darted through the front doors with the marines
close behind. Silence gestured for the two marines to
spread out, and they did so quickly and pro-
fessionally. The esper looked round the empty Lobby
and hugged herself, possibly from the cold.

The Reception desk was unmanned, its Security
monitor screens blank. Papers lay scattered across the
desk, covered with a thin layer of frost. Silence
gestured for the two marines to check the desk, and
they moved forward, guns at the ready. Investigator
Frost looked unhurriedly about her, trying to get the

feel of the place. There was no sign of any panic or fight. Everything was still in its place, just as it had been left. At the desk, Stasiak studied the scattered papers without touching them. They were all routine, everyday stuff, and Stasiak thought there was something sad in that. The people who worked here had got no warning, no chance to prepare themselves. They probably thought it was just another day, until the boom fell, and the lights started going out. He looked at Ripper, who was trying to get the Security monitors back on line, with no success. He straightened up with a sigh, looked at Silence, and shook his head.

'Not a thing, Captain. There's power in the system somewhere, but it's not reaching Reception. I think it's being diverted somewhere else, but don't ask me where.'

'Not a damn thing to go on,' said Stasiak. 'It's as though everyone just . . . got up and left. Spooky.'

'Look around, see if you can turn up some lamps or torches,' said Silence. 'We're not going to get far without some light. Investigator; try the comm net. Maybe we can raise someone, now that we're actually inside the Base.'

Frost nodded, and activated her comm implant. 'This is Investigator Frost, of the *Darkwind*. Please respond.'

They all listened, but there was only the low hum of an open channel.

'Can anybody hear me? This is Investigator Frost. I speak for the Empire. Respond, please.'

She frowned suddenly as a voice murmured in her ear, so soft and faint the words were indistinguishable. Frost looked quickly at the others, but though they'd all heard it too, none of them could make it out either. Frost boosted the volume as high as it would go, but the voice had stopped.

'I hear you,' she said clearly. 'Please say again. Where are you? Do you require assistance?'

There was no reply. Frost turned the volume back down, looked at Silence and shook her head. He turned to Diana.

'Run a full scan, esper. If there's anything alive and thinking in this place, I want to know what and where it is.'

Diana turned away so he couldn't see her face. She'd been waiting for him to ask, and wondering what she would do when he did. All her training, all her conditioning, made it impossible for her to disobey a direct order, but she still remembered the horror she'd encountered the last time she'd raised her esp. She remembered the screaming voices, human voices, and the terrible presence that had looked back at her with knowing, hungry eyes. In all her years, she'd never seen anything that scared her more. And now Silence wanted her to open her mind to it. She couldn't. She just couldn't. But she couldn't refuse, either. She closed her eyes and opened her esp just a fraction, like a child peering warily between raised fingers. Everything was still and quiet. She probed a little further, letting her mind drift cautiously out across the ground floor, but there was nothing there. She sighed inwardly with relief, and looked at Silence again.

'No trace of life anywhere, Captain. There's always the chance that something's blocking my esp, but if there is, I can't detect it.'

She waited breathlessly while he considered her answer, expecting him any moment to glare at her coldly as he saw through her half-truth, but he just nodded and turned away, and she didn't know whether to feel relieved or ashamed.

Silence frowned thoughtfully. 'Odin; give me the floor plans for Base Thirteen, on an overlay. One floor at a time, starting with the ground floor. And patch the others in too.'

A schematic appeared before him, superimposed on his vision. It seemed fairly straightforward. Only the one entrance to the ground floor, and one elevator and two sets of stairs leading down to the next floors. All Bases were built downwards into the earth, for greater security. Everything important was on the bottom floor, Level Three, protected by thick concrete and other, less obvious, measures. Silence studied the layout for each floor, checking particularly for entrances and exits, and then had Odin dismiss the overlay.

'All right, people; pay attention. It looks like we're
going to have to do this the hard way. I'm splitting us
into two groups, so we can cover more ground.
Carrion, Frost; you stay with me. We'll search this
floor. Esper; you and the two marines start checking
out the next floor down. Take your time and check
every room thoroughly before you go on to the next.
Don't take any chances, and yell for help if you spot
anything that looks even remotely threatening. I want
information, not dead heroes. And whatever happens; no one is to go off on their own. Understood?'
There was a general murmur of assent and nodding
of heads. 'All right then, people; let's make a start. By
the book and by the numbers.'

The marines sketched a quick salute, turned on
one of the emergency lamps Ripper had found
tucked away behind the Reception desk, and set off
towards the rear stairwell marked on the floor plan.
Diana hurried after them, not liking the idea of
investigating the next floor down, but liking the idea
of being left behind and alone even less.

Frost turned on her lamp. The light was bright and
cheerful, though it raised uneasy shadows at the
corner of everyone's eyes. Frost offered the lamp to
Carrion, but he shook his head courteously. Silence
took it from her, and led the two of them off into the
gloom of the ground floor.

Corridor by corridor, room by room, they pro-
gressed slowly but everywhere was quiet and

deserted, with no sign of any struggle or disturbance. Computer panels were unlit, monitor screens were dark, but there was still evidence of the people who'd lived and worked in Base Thirteen. An open message pad, a half-completed form, a cup almost full of coffee. Silence picked up the cup. There was a thick layer of frozen scum on the surface of the coffee. He put it down almost angrily. Still no signs of trouble, or even surprise. Whatever happened, it must have been quick. The thought was not comforting. Base Thirteen should have been crawling with Security personnel and back-up emergency systems, even if Unseeli was supposed to be a dead world. The Empire didn't believe in taking chances. But somehow the aliens had got into the Base, taken over its systems and dealt with its personnel, all without being detected or challenged. Which was supposed to be impossible.

'Interesting,' said Carrion.

'What?' said Frost, looking quickly about her.

'Your gun,' said Carrion. 'I hadn't looked at it before. I don't recognise it.'

Frost shrugged. 'Standard disrupter. I suppose the style's changed a lot in the past ten years. This version is far superior to the old model.'

'Really. What's the recharge time?'

'Got it down to three minutes now.'

Carrion raised an eyebrow. 'That is an improvement, I see you still carry a sword.'

'Of course.' Frost grinned. 'A sword never needs recharging.'

'Your attention, please,' said Odin suddenly through their comm implants. 'I have discovered something important, Captain. Apparently Commander Starblood had been concerned about possible intruders in the Base even before the alien ship crashed. There are several references in his log to sightings of "ghosts", or some kind of presence, by Base personnel. These sightings were so frequent and so worrying that Commander Starblood became quite disturbed by them. So disturbed he ordered six Security Guardians. There's a record of their delivery, two weeks before the alien ship's arrival.'

Silence scowled. 'Six Guardians? How the hell did the aliens get past them?'

'What exactly are Guardians?' said Carrion.

'After your time,' said Frost. 'They're state-of-the-art Security robots. Fast, powerful, efficient, and a really nasty attitude. They were designed originally for riot control. One per riot. And Starblood ordered six . . . He must have been really scared. Six would have been enough to stand off a small army.'

'And if they're still here, and running loose,' said Silence, 'we are in real trouble.'

CHAPTER SEVEN

Guardians

The marines moved cautiously down the metal stairway, scowling into the gloom below. The guns in their hands swept constantly back and forth, covering every direction an attack could come from. Diana supposed she should find such obvious expertise comforting, but instead it just reminded her of the possible dangers ahead. It almost made her wish she carried a gun of her own. Almost. She was an esper, not a killer. She stuck as close behind the marines as she could without crowding them, holding her lamp high to spread its light as far as possible. Huge shadows moved around them like watching ghosts, but everything else was still and silent.

They'd found an elevator that could have taken them down to the next floor, but none of them had felt like risking it. They had no idea why it was still working when so many other things weren't, and it was only too easy to imagine the elevator breaking down between floors, leaving them trapped in a steel coffin while the air ran out. So they made their way slowly down the stairs, nerves tingling in anticipation of an attack that never came.

It was cold in the stairwell, and getting colder. Hoarfrost made patterns on the walls that teased the eye with hints of meaning. Their breath steamed on the still air, and the heating elements in their uniforms somehow weren't enough to keep the chill out of their bones. Their footsteps rang loudly on the metal steps, and the sound seemed to echo unnaturally long in the hush.

Diana knew she should be using her esp to check ahead, but she couldn't bring herself to do that. Not yet. The scan in the Lobby had been hard enough, when she was safe and among friends. But now that she'd come down into the heart of the darkness, she was afraid to send her mind out for fear it might not come back. She sensed there was something down there in the dark with them, and she didn't want to risk waking it again. Sometimes she thought it was an alien, and sometimes she thought it might be the ghosts of dead personnel, but all she really knew for sure was that she was scared. So scared that even the awful forms her imagination conjured up were preferable to encountering the real thing again. It was safer to lie to herself and hide in the dark with the marines.

They finally reached the bottom of the stairwell, and stood close together at the foot of the steps. To their right, a thick coating of ice almost covered the sign saying 'Level Two'. The marines and the esper ignored it, their gaze fixed on what the esper's lamplight revealed before them. The corridor walls bulged and seethed with ugly alien growths, and thick strands of shimmering webbing hung down from the ceiling, twisting and turning slowly as though in response to an unfelt breeze. The metal walls had torn and split apart in many places, multi-coloured wiring hanging out like plastic viscera, as though the alien forms had somehow grown inside the walls, and burst out when they'd become too large to be contained. Silvery traces ran along the unbroken areas of wall in long enigmatic patterns, gleaming brightly in the lamplight like metallic veins. They were pulsing with a slow alien life. The whole ceiling was covered with dark, wart-like nodes the size of a man's head, surrounded and connected by swirling chalky white spirals. And thick on the air, a harsh sweet smell like a disturbed grave.

'What the hell is this?' breathed Stasiak, swinging his gun back and forth, unable to settle on a single target. 'The place looks . . . diseased.'

'Infested, anyway,' said Ripper. 'I think we can be sure now that the aliens came here after they left their ship.' He glanced at the esper beside him. 'This . . . mixture of living and unliving; is this the same kind of thing you found on the alien ship?'

The esper had to swallow hard before she could answer, but when she finally spoke her voice was cool and quite professional. 'The same kind of thing, yes. Only the ship was dead, or dying. This looks alive, and functioning. The alien crew must have brought it with them, as some kind of seed, perhaps. But why? Surely they didn't bring about changes as extensive as this just so that they could feel at home? There must be a purpose to it.'

'If there is, it's an alien purpose,' said Ripper. 'Something we might not even recognise, let alone understand. I think we need the Investigator down here to check this out, before we go any further.'

'Wait a minute,' said Stasiak quickly. 'Let's think about this first. We don't need to know what this stuff is. It looks weird and smells worse, but it's not exactly aggressive, is it? We're supposed to be looking for the Base personnel, and we don't need Frost for that. We're marines; we can handle this without an Investigator to hold our hands.'

Ripper looked at Stasiak thoughtfully. 'This isn't like you, Lou. It's an improvement, but it isn't like you. What are you up to?'

Stasiak grinned. 'Odin's recording everything that happens here, remember? And you can bet a lot of high-up people are going to be studying this record. This is our chance to look good in front of people who matter, and do ourselves no harm in the process. Why let Frost steal all the glory? There's money and fame in this; I can smell it. Of course, we'll have to edit this bit out . . .'

'People have died here,' said Diana sharply. 'And all you can think of is how best to turn it to your own advantage?'

Stasiak shrugged. 'If they're already dead, there's not much left I can do for them. So we might as well help ourselves, while we can.'

'And if whatever killed these people finds us?'

'Then we avenge the dead,' said Ripper. 'We know our duty, Diana. We're marines.'

Diana sniffed, and looked away, ostensibly studying the alien scene before her. Ripper shrugged. 'Odin; are you getting all this?'

'I see everything you see,' murmured the AI in his ear. 'It's really most fascinating. Please proceed further into the changed area. I need more information on the extent of the changes.'

'Wait a minute,' said Stasiak immediately. 'There's no point in rushing on blindly. There could be all kinds of unpleasantness up ahead.'

Ripper looked at him amused. 'A minute ago you were all for plunging into the thick of it, in search of death or glory.'

'I'm ambitious, not crazy. Let's handle this nice and easy, one step at a time. The only good hero is the kind who survives to talk about merchandising.'

And then he broke off, and they all looked round sharply as a single echoing thud came out of the darkness ahead of them. It sounded heavy and threatening and quite deliberate, as though whatever was responsible for the sound had wanted it to be heard. Ripper and Stasiak levelled their disrupters on the corridor ahead. Diana's right hand went to the force-shield bracelet on her left wrist, but hesitated to activate it. The energy crystal that powered it had a limited life span, and she didn't want to use it up unnecessarily.

'Odin; can your sensors detect anything alive on this floor?' said Ripper quietly.

'I'm afraid my sensors are currently unable to penetrate the Base,' the AI said quietly. 'Something is blocking them. My only sources of information are what I see and hear through your comm implants.'

More noises came out of the darkness, a slow regular thudding like the beating of a giant heart. The floor vibrated beneath their feet in time to the rhythm, and something large and hulking came out of the gloom towards them. It was huge, filling the corridor, and Diana shrank back, a child again, frightened by the bogeyman in the dark. The figure stopped suddenly a dozen feet away, its blue steel exterior glinting in the shaking lamplight. Its bent head scraped against the ceiling, and its metal hands were studded with razors. Stasiak swore softly, but his hand was steady as he turned his disrupter on the figure.

Captain Silence's voice rang suddenly in their ears. 'Listen up, people. We have a problem. Odin tells me there are Security Guardians somewhere in the Base.

Don't engage them, under any circumstances. It's very possible they've been programmed to protect this Base against intruders. If you see one, retreat immediately.'

'Thanks for the warning,' said Ripper. 'But it's just a bit late. We're looking at one right now. Please advise.'

'Get the hell out of there,' said Silence immediately. 'Make no threatening moves and back away. If it starts towards you, run. They're crawling with weaponry and they don't take prisoners. As long as you keep a fair distance away, you should be safe.'

'Should?' said Stasiak. 'What do you mean, should? I'm not moving a muscle until I'm sure it's safe.'

'Shut up, Lou,' said Ripper. 'Esper; back away, and start up the stairs. We'll follow you.'

'All right,' said Diana quietly. 'I'm starting now.'

She stepped back cautiously, and the huge figure raised a hand to point at her. A disrupter beam flew from a finger and blew apart the metal stairway in a rain of jagged shrapnel.

Cries and screams and obscenities burst from Silence's comm implant, drowned out almost immediately by the sound of an explosion from below. The noise was deafening, and the floor shook briefly. Carrion and Frost looked to Silence for orders.

'Whatever's happening down there, there's nothing

we can do,' he said flatly. 'By the time we could get there it would all be over, one way or another. And the last thing we want to do is provide a Guardian with new targets. Esper, marines; can you hear me? Fall back. I repeat, fall back.' He waited, but there was no reply, only the quiet hum of an open comm channel. 'Odin; access what they're seeing and patch me in.'

'I'm sorry, Captain,' said the AI steadily. 'Something inside the Base is interfering with the comm network. I have lost all visual contact with the esper and the marines. I am still monitoring audio signals, but I can't be sure how long that will last. I strongly advise that you leave Base Thirteen now. You are not equipped to deal with Guardians.'

'Want to bet?' drawled Frost. 'Point me at one. Anything that gets in my way is going to regret it.'

Carrion looked at Silence. 'Is she always this confident?'

'Yes,' said Silence. 'Frightening, isn't it?'

Carrion looked away suddenly. 'Captain . . . something's coming. Something close.'

Frost and Silence drew their guns and covered the two approaches. The wide corridor was still and open, with doors leading off at both sides. The only light came from the lamp Silence was holding, a pale illumination just strong enough to show both ends of the corridor. Nothing moved, but the shadows had edges. What had been just another corridor was suddenly openly menacing, every doorway a threat. Silence and Frost moved to stand back to back. Carrion leaned on his staff, frowning, as though listening to something only he could hear. Silence strained his ears against the hush, but couldn't catch anything.

'What is it?' he said quietly to the outlaw. 'Which direction is it coming from?'

Carrion's eyes closed. 'They're here, Captain. They're here.'

The wall to their right tore apart like paper as the Guardian burst through into the corridor. Thick strands of coloured wiring fouled one arm, but the Guardian snapped them with one easy movement. The machine was eight feet tall, a broad metal colossus with glowing eyes and a constant unnerving grin on its blue steel face. Razored blades protruded from its arms and legs, and the knuckles on its hands were spiked. It was not alive, but hate and violence were a part of its nature. It was a killing machine, fashioned in the shape of a man because it was more frightening that way.

'Big, isn't it?' said Carrion.

The sound of heavy metal footsteps rang out at both ends of the corridor, and two more Guardians appeared, blocking off the only means of escape. The three machines stood unnaturally still, studying their targets, and then they surged forward, too fast for the human eye to follow. Silence aimed and fired his

disrupter at the nearest Guardian as it emerged from
the wreckage of the wall. A force shield snapped on
just in time to deflect the energy bolt, and then
disappeared. The machine raised a hand and pointed,
and Silence threw himself to one side as an energy
beam blew a hole in the wall where he'd been
standing. Silence hit the floor rolling, and was quickly
back on his feet again. He slapped the metal bracelet
on his left wrist, and a force shield sprang into being
on his left arm. A yard-long oblong of glowing energy,
it was capable of deflecting any energy weapon. For
as long as it lasted. The Guardian could turn its shield
on and off with split-second timing, so that it lasted
practically for ever. Silence didn't have that option.
He also had another three minutes to wait before he
could use his gun again, and the Guardian was right
on top of him.

Silence kicked open the door to his left, darted into
the room and slammed the door shut behind him.
He didn't really think it was going to stop something
that could crash through walls, but hoped it would
buy him a little time while he worked on what the
hell to do next. A metal fist punched a hole in the
door. Silence watched, fascinated, as an arm followed
the hand through the hole, and then the Guardian
pulled it back sharply, yanking the door out of its
frame. The Guardian stepped unhurriedly into the
room, widening the doorway as it did so. Silence
backed away, holding his shield up before him.

The corridor was plunged into darkness as Silence disappeared into the side room, taking the only lamp with him. Frost cursed dispassionately and switched to her infra-red implants, only to discover the Guardians were shielded against displaying any heat signs. She immediately switched to ambient light and activated her force shield. The shield's glow was more than enough to show her the Guardian advancing on her. Frost fired her gun, but the energy bolt glanced harmlessly from the machine's force shield. She shrugged calmly, put her gun away, and drew a knife from inside her boot. It was viciously wide and almost a foot long, and its edges looked blurred and uncertain.

'Monofilament edge,' said Frost to Carrion. 'Cut through anything. Have to be careful with it, though, or it'll have your fingers off.'

'Those things were illegal, in my day,' observed Carrion.

'They still are. But I won't tell anyone if you won't.'

And then the Guardians were upon them, and there was no more time for talk. Frost threw herself forward, and the knife lashed out to cut a chunk off a Guardian's hand. The built-in disrupters all fired at once, but her force shield protected her. Frost brought the energy field across sideways, and its razor-sharp edge sliced clean through the other hand as it reached for her. The Guardian's huge metal arms swept suddenly in, to hold her in a bear hug and crush her against the blades on its chest. Frost dropped to her knees and rolled to one side, and the great arms closed on nothing. She jumped back, scrambling quickly to regain her feet, and the Guardian went after her, reaching for her with its crippled hands.

Frost darted in and out, slashing at the Guardian with her knife, cutting and carving it, but unable to do any real damage. It was just too big, and her knife was too small. The machine's computer-enhanced moves were inhumanly fast, and only her Investigator's training enabled her to avoid it. And she knew she couldn't maintain that kind of speed for long. She could turn and run. The Guardian didn't look like it was built for high-speed pursuit. But that would mean abandoning Carrion and the Captain, and her duty. Investigators didn't run away. She darted in under the Guardian's reach, pushed her gun against its chest and pressed the stud. Nothing happened. There hadn't been enough time for the energy crystal to recharge. She scrambled up the Guardian, climbing it like a cat, and dropped to the ground behind it. She spun round quickly, and stabbed the machine in the back before it could turn. It shuddered once, but that was all. The knife wasn't long enough to reach the parts that mattered. She yanked the blade out, and a metal arm whirled round and sent her flying down the corridor. She'd had her force shield up in time, but the impact was still enough to knock the breath out of her. She got her feet under her and backed away as the Guardian advanced on her, implacable and unstoppable as death itself.

Carrion had crouched down, and frozen where he was when Silence disappeared with the lamp. In the dark, the Guardian could only track him by sound. Unless the damn thing had infra red too. And then Frost turned on her force shield, and Carrion's long-neglected eye enhancements kicked in, boosting the ambient light. Carrion straightened up as he saw the third Guardian advancing on him. He drew his power about him, crackling and sparking on the air, and reached out to tear the machine apart. But his power dropped away and was gone in an instant. Carrion stood for a moment, staring blankly, and that was almost enough to get himself killed. The Guardian raised its arm, and all the disrupters in the hand fired at once. Carrion threw himself to one side at the last moment, old combat reflexes coming to his rescue. The damn thing had psi inhibitors built into it. They worked on the opposite principle to his own power lance, dampening down psi energy instead of augmenting it. The Empire used them to keep espers in line. They reacted to build-ups in psionic energy and cut in automatically once it rose above a certain level. Carrion backed away from the Guardian, holding his useless power lance out before him.

The Guardian loomed over him, reaching for him with razored hands. Carrion reached inside himself and drew on his power. The psi inhibitors prevented him from doing anything dramatic, but it was surprising what you could do with even small amounts. He reached out with his mind, a whisper of psychokinesis almost too small to register, and slipped it deftly between the Guardian's feet and the floor. All friction vanished in a moment as he concentrated, and the Guardian's feet shot out from under it. It fell on its back with a deafening crash, and Carrion quickly reached out to do the same to the machine threatening Frost. It hit the floor hard, and Frost stepped forward and drove her monofilament knife into its gleaming skull. The Guardian jerked and trembled, and lay twitching on its back on the floor. Frost pulled the knife out and calmly set about sawing the grinning head off.

The wall to Carrion's left exploded, throwing shrapnel across the corridor, and Carrion had to put up his esper screen to protect himself. He couldn't concentrate on that and the Guardian, and the machine rose quickly to its feet again. Silence clambered through the hole in the wall. A metal hand reached out after him, and Silence threw himself forward to avoid it. He scrambled away to stand beside Carrion, breathing hard. The Guardian before them fired a disrupter, and Silence blocked it with his force shield, holding it at an angle so that the beam glanced off and struck the Guardian that was climbing through the hole in the wall. It stopped the beam with a force shield, but was slowed for a moment.

Silence grinned breathlessly. 'Same trick I used to make that thing provide me with an exit through the wall.'

'Very clever,' said Carrion. 'Almost as clever as disappearing into another room and taking the only light with you.'

'Ah,' said Silence. 'Sorry about that. It's been a while since I did any hand-to-hand stuff. I'm rather out of practice.'

They jumped in different directions as Carrion's Guardian fired once more, and the vivid energy beam flashed past them down the corridor to blow a hole in the far wall. Silence's Guardian crashed out into the corridor again, shaking off encumbering debris, and turned to face Frost. She hefted the severed metal head in her hand, and threw it at the machine. It caught the head easily, put it down on the floor with surprising gentleness, and started towards the Investigator. She grinned at it unpleasantly, her knife held out before her. And then the headless machine on the floor behind her reached out and grabbed her firmly by the ankle.

Carrion raised his esp as high as he dared, focused his psychokinesis tightly, and punched a hole right through the chest of the Guardian before him. It shuddered under the impact, but did not fall. The outlaw retreated, Silence at his side.

'Is there any way of beating these things?' said Carrion.

'Not really, no,' said Silence. 'I'm amazed we lasted this long. They're supposed to be unstoppable. But then, that's never bothered you before.'

And then the Guardian was upon them, and there was no more time for words.

Diana crouched down behind her force shield, trembling violently as the Guardians advanced on her. The two marines had already fired their disrupters, to no effect, and were also reduced to hiding behind their force shields and looking frantically around for a way out. The Guardians strode unwaveringly through the alien-infested corridor, ignoring everything except their targets. Ripper pulled a grenade from his belt, primed it, and tossed it into the midst of the three machines. It blew a second later, and the corridor filled with alien fragments and thick, choking smoke. Stasiak grabbed Diana's wrist and hauled her after him as he and Ripper ran down a side corridor, away from the smoke and the undamaged Guardians, already striding through the smoke after them.

The alien changes became stranger and more overpowering as they fled deeper into Level Two, but Diana was too busy coughing the smoke out of her lungs to pay much attention to her surroundings. Tears were streaming down her face, as much from shock as the smoke. She'd never seen anything so obviously deadly and efficient as the Guardians. They scared her on some basic, primal level that left no room in her for anything but flight. The Guardians were everything about the Empire that had ever threatened or punished her; brute symbols of authority, relentless as justice or revenge. She could no more have raised a hand against them than she could have defied her own conditioning.

The marines' pace slowed as they left the smoke behind them, but they could still hear the Guardians not far behind them. Stasiak produced a small capsule from somewhere and swallowed it dry, grimacing at the effort. He offered one to Ripper, who got his down more easily. Stasiak grinned at Diana, his eyes already bright and glassy.

'Just a little something, to give a fighting man an edge. You want one?' Diana shook her head. She didn't trust battle drugs. Stasiak shrugged and pulled her on. 'Up to you. But don't slow us down, or I'll have to leave you. Right, Rip?'

Ripper nodded brusquely, without looking round, and Diana fought to keep up with them as they made their way down a corridor distorted by strange alien growths. The hanging streamers of webbing grew steadily thicker, clinging stickily to the marines and the esper as they pushed through them. The corridor grew narrower, pressing in uncomfortably from all sides as the alien growths ran wild. It seemed to Diana that they'd left the Base behind, and were running through a harsh new world. But the Guardians were still following. She could hear them. The changing nature of their surroundings didn't seem to be slowing them at all. And then a side corridor ended in a great swollen mass of tissue, and there was no point in running any more. The marines cut at the spongy mass with their swords, but it absorbed their blows with easy indifference. They turned and glared back down the corridor. Stasiak swallowed another capsule. The sound of approaching metal footsteps came clearly on the quiet.

Ripper tapped Stasiak on the arm and gestured upwards. Stasiak frowned, and then his face cleared as Ripper hefted his gun. They aimed their disrupters at the ceiling, at the point where the Guardians would enter the side corridor. Diana stood behind them, her force shield humming loudly on the quiet, and tried to control her trembling. And then the Guardians appeared at the end of the corridor, and Stasiak and Ripper fired at the ceiling above them.

The growths exploded and the ceiling blew apart. Fat sparks flew on the air as electrical systems fused and failed, and half the floor above collapsed on to the Guardians, burying them under tons of rubble. The marines and the esper watched in silence as the wreckage slowly settled, and then Diana surprised herself with a loud whoop of glee. The marines laughed and whooped a few times themselves. They all turned off their force shields and hugged each other, almost giddy from relief. And then they fell silent as the wreckage shifted. Broken metal and ragged tissues stirred and fell back as a Guardian rose slowly from the debris. Its blue steel exterior was barely scratched.

The Guardian advanced unhurriedly on Silence and Carrion. It knew there was nowhere they could go. If they tried to run it would shoot them, and if they stood their ground and tried to hide behind their force shields, it would tear them apart. At the other end of the corridor, the Guardian Frost had beheaded was clinging firmly to her ankle, while the third Guardian advanced on her. Silence looked desperately at Carrion.

'Do something! Use your lance!'

'If I try the same trick again, the psi inhibitors will stop me,' said Carrion calmly. 'If I persist, they'll burn my brain out.'

Silence backed slowly away and Carrion moved back with him. The Guardian lifted its hands to cover them with its disrupters. Silence thought furiously. The damn things had to have a weakness somewhere. Everything had a weak point. Except the Guardians had been designed to be unstoppable. Inhumanly strong, computer-fast reflexes ... computers. Silence seized on that thought. The Guardians were part of the Base's Security systems, which meant they were run by the Security computers ...

'Odin! Can you hear me?'

'Yes, Captain. Audio contact remains firm.'

'Patch into the Base Security computers and shut them down! Shut down anything that even looks like it might be running a Guardian!'

'Of course, Captain. An excellent stratagem.' There was a slight pause, and then the AI's voice returned. 'I regret I am unable to comply, Captain. I am unable to find any computer system still functioning in Base Thirteen capable of running a Guardian. Only a few emergency systems are still functioning.'

'What?' Silence looked blankly at Carrion. 'But if the computers aren't running the Guardians . . . they must be running themselves. And that's not possible. That's not possible!'

'Are you going to tell them that, or shall I?' said Carrion.

'Damnit, do something, Carrion! That thing will kill both of us!'

'Yes,' said the outlaw quietly. 'I think it will, Captain.'

At the other end of the corridor, Frost pried desperately at the steel fingers gripping her ankle. The other Guardian was almost on top of her, but she couldn't break the hold. She snarled silently and cut savagely at the metal arm, slicing through its wrist. She threw herself clumsily to one side, dodging the reaching hands, and got her feet under her again. The severed hand was still gripping her ankle fiercely.

Which meant she had no chance of outrunning her opponent, but then, she wasn't the running kind. She slashed at the advancing Guardian with her mono-filament knife, and the blade bounced harmlessly back from the machine's force field. Frost shrugged quickly, and darted back out of reach. It seemed the Guardians were capable of learning from experience. Actually, she was surprised she'd lasted this long. She cut the metal hand from her ankle with a few quick slashes from the knife, and then had to throw herself to one side as disrupter beams seared through the air where she'd been standing. She hit the floor rolling, and was quickly back on her feet and dodging more disrupter shots.

A thought kept nagging at her, even as she dodged and ducked. The Guardians were fast, but they weren't anywhere near as fast as she'd expected them to be. As they were supposed to be. In fact, it was just possible that she was faster than they were. Which gave her an idea. The Guardians had force shields, but they were only using them to deflect disrupter beams. Apparently they didn't see anything else as a big enough threat. Frost grinned unpleasantly, and pulled a concussion grenade from her bandolier. She ducked another disrupter blast, leapt past the Guard-ian, and jumped on to the back of the headless Guardian as it peered blindly about for its prey. She primed the grenade, stuffed it into the open neck and leapt away. There was a muffled explosion, and smoke poured from the open neck, but the Guardian didn't go down. Frost stared at it incredulously. How much punishment could these things take?

Silence and Carrion edged away from the advancing Guardian until they backed into a wall, and there was nowhere left to go. Carrion looked at Silence.

'I seem to have run out of options, Captain. If you have any last-minute master plan, I think this would be a good time to share it.'

'Sorry,' said Silence. 'I was depending on you.'

Carrion managed something that was almost a smile. 'You should have known better than that, John.'

Frost turned from the headless Guardian before her, and stumbled over the severed head itself. She glanced down automatically, and stopped as something caught her eye. Without slowing her cautious retreat, she snatched up the head and studied it more closely. The headless machine hesitated, and then stopped where it was. The other Guardian stopped too. Frost blinked, puzzled, and took a better look at the detached head. The light had gone out of its eyes, though it still wore its endless disturbing grin, but there was something about it ... She turned it over in her hands, still keeping a wary eye on the motionless Guardians, and then whistled soundlessly as she saw the interior of the head. A great many things suddenly became clear. Where there should have been nothing but silicon circuitry and crystalline

matrixes, there were also thick strands of living tissue.
Alien tissue.

She looked down the corridor, and saw that the
third Guardian had stopped its advance on Silence
and Carrion. She called out to them and tossed the
head in their direction. It bumped and rolled across
the uneven floor, and the Guardians made no move
to intercept it. Finally it rolled to a halt, and Silence
reached carefully down and picked it up. He raised
an eyebrow at the inside of the head, and showed it
to Carrion.

'Interesting,' said Carrion.

'Explains a lot, doesn't it?' said Silence. 'No wonder
they didn't need the Security computers to run them.
The aliens invaded them too. The damn things are
alive . . .'

'And now that we know, that changes a lot of
things,' said Carrion. 'There wasn't much my esp
could do against standard Guardians without trigger-
ing the psi inhibitors, but living tissue is much more
responsive to esper attack . . .'

He looked at the Guardian before him, and it began
to shudder, as though it was cold, or afraid. It
dropped to its knees, fell forward on to its grinning
face, and lay still. Carrion looked at the two remaining
Guardians, and they collapsed like puppets whose
strings had been cut. Rather an appropriate meta-
phor, Silence decided. Of course, where there were

puppets, there were also puppeteers. They still had to face whatever it was that had infested the Base.

Frost made her way over to them, and kicked the nearest Guardian dismissively. 'Is that it? I'm almost disappointed it was so easy.'

'Don't worry,' said Carrion. 'I doubt very much that our troubles are over yet.'

'Right,' said Silence. 'The whole Base must be riddled with this stuff. If we can't find a way to clean it out, we may have to abandon the Base and destroy it from orbit.'

'The Empire wouldn't like that,' said Carrion.

'No,' said Frost. 'It wouldn't.'

Silence looked sharply at Carrion. 'Hold everything; we're forgetting the esper and the marines. We haven't had a word from them since we lost contact.'

'Don't worry,' said Carrion. 'I've just contacted Diana. It seems they had Guardian troubles of their own. I've explained what needs to be done. The esper is quite capable of handling the Guardians herself.'

Down on Level Two, Diana Vertue looked smugly at the Guardians lying motionless among the wreckage of the ceiling. The marines took it in turns to clap her on the back, almost knocking her off her feet in the process.

'Mind you, this is just Level Two,' said Stasiak.

'I hate to think what might be waiting for us down on Level Three.'

Ripper nodded and looked at Diana. 'You'd better run a scan, see if there are any more like these waiting below.'

She nodded, closed her eyes, and let her mind drift cautiously up and out. She frowned almost immediately.

'What is it?' said Stasiak.

'Living traces,' said Diana. 'They're all around us, all over the Base, concentrated in the floor below. They know we're here.' Her voice rose suddenly. 'They're not hiding from us any more. They're coming for us.'

'Who?' said Stasiak, glaring wildly about him. 'Who's coming for us?'

The walls around them burst apart, thick metal tearing like paper, as alien growths and tentacles exploded into the corridor, reaching for the esper and the two marines. The tentacles came from the floor and the walls and the ceiling, and there was nowhere to hide from them.

CHAPTER EIGHT

Down in the Darkness

'Esper; can you hear me? Ripper, Stasiak; respond!'
Silence waited, scowling, but there was no response.
He looked into the stairwell that led down to Level
Two, and the darkness looked back at him, arrogant
and impenetrable. There was only the cold and the
quiet, and the knowledge of what he'd have to do. It
had been twenty minutes now, since Carrion had last
been able to reach the esper. He'd told her how to
handle the Guardians, and she'd acknowledged the
message, but there'd been nothing since. Silence
shook his head slowly. They couldn't be dead. They
had the information they needed. They couldn't be
dead.

'Odin; could something be interfering with the
comm net?'

'Quite possibly, Captain,' the AI murmured in his
ear. 'I have been unable to raise the party on Level
Two for some time. Something in Base Thirteen is
interfering with all levels of communication. I am
having to use inordinate amounts of power just to
maintain audio contact with your party. However,

that would not explain the outlaw's inability to contact them with his mind.'

'We have to go down after them,' said Frost, holding her lamp out over the gloom in the stairwell. Shadows leapt and danced, giving away nothing. 'If something has happened to the others, we need to know what it is.'

'Whatever's happened, the odds are it's over by now,' said Carrion. 'We won't do anyone any good by rushing blindly into the dark. Wait a moment, and consider. So far, we have a growing number of questions, and few if any good answers. For example; if Base Commander Starblood had six Security Guardians at his disposal, why didn't he use them against the invading aliens?'

'Presumably because he didn't have time,' said Frost. 'Judging by his log entries, by the time he'd worked out what was happening it was already too late. In fact, it's entirely possible the Guardians were infested with the alien material before they could be deployed.'

'Exactly,' said Carrion, leaning elegantly on his staff. 'The aliens aren't just powerful and dangerous, they're fast and devious too. All of which suggests we'd be foolish to go rushing into an unknown situation without doing some hard thinking first. The more I think about it, the more this looks to me like a trap, with the esper and the marines as bait.'

'You're probably right,' said Silence. 'But it doesn't

make any difference. Those are my people down there, and I won't put their lives at risk by holding back. Lead the way, Investigator; Carrion and I will be right behind you.'

Frost grinned quickly, a sudden flash of bared teeth, and started down the metal stairs, lamp in one hand, gun in the other. Carrion gave Silence a long, thoughtful look, and then followed the Investigator down into the blackness. Silence brought up the rear. The stairwell was narrow and confined, and the lamplight didn't travel far. They moved in a small pool of light, and shadows flickered menacingly around them, almost close enough to touch. They'd barely reached the half-way mark when Frost stopped suddenly, and Carrion and Silence almost bumped into her. She stood still, head cocked slightly to one side, listening.

'What is it, Investigator?' said Silence quietly.

'I'm not sure, Captain. I heard something; something close.'

She broke off sharply, and held the lamp down to light her feet. A yard-long insect with a broad carapaced back and hundreds of legs was curling itself unhurriedly round her left ankle. Dozens more of the things curled and twisted on the steps below. More were climbing the walls, clinging easily to the dull metal. Frost put away her gun and drew her sword, moving slowly and carefully. The creature had no eyes or mouth, but she set the edge of her blade against what seemed to be the front of the insect, and sliced sideways. The body convulsed, and clamped painfully tight around her ankle. Frost handed the lamp to Carrion, reached down and calmly tackled the insect on her leg. It fought back with surprising strength, even without its head, and she had to use all her strength to unwrap it. It finally came free, and immediately tried to wrap itself around her arm. She threw the thing away, and it disappeared into the darkness. Hundreds more seethed on the steps below her, scuttling and sliding over each other in their eagerness to get to their new prey.

Carrion tossed the lamp lightly into the air and held it there with his esp, spreading light over the scene and keeping his hands free. Silence aimed his disrupter where the mass of insects seemed the thickest.

'I wouldn't, Captain,' said the outlaw quietly. 'You'd do more damage to the stairs than to the creatures.'

Silence nodded stiffly, and put away his gun. He shouldn't have needed to be told something that obvious. He drew his sword and stepped carefully down beside the Investigator. Together they hacked and cut at the insects, clearing an open space before them. Segments flew on the air, legs still kicking, but the creatures wouldn't die. They pressed blindly forward up the stairs, seeking to wrap themselves round an arm or a leg, reaching always for the throat, as though somehow they knew that to be the most vulnerable spot. They climbed the walls and dropped on to the party from above, but Carrion deflected them with his esp, cracking them like whips to break their backs, or crushing them against the walls with the pressure of his mind. But still the insects pressed forward, and there seemed no end to them.

Carrion stepped back, and held his staff horizontally above his head. Psi energy spat and crackled at each end of the power lance, and stabbed out to strike at the seething creatures. Where the psi-bolts struck the insects burst into flames, curling and twisting as the fire consumed them. Energy danced back and forth in the stairwell, too bright to look at, scorching and crisping the scuttling creatures, but not touching Silence or the Investigator. The insects fell back, spilling down the stairs in desperate haste, and plunged into the solid steel walls, which accepted and swallowed them up in a moment. The insects disappeared into the walls as though the gleaming steel was insubstantial as mist, and were quickly gone. Within seconds the stairwell was empty, the sound of the insects' scuttling feet no more than a swiftly fading echo. Only the dead remained to show that they had ever been there. Frost reached out and tapped the nearest wall, but it was stubbornly solid to the touch.

'Interesting,' said Carrion, and the Investigator nodded.

'Is that all you've got to say?' demanded Silence.

'For the moment,' said Carrion. 'The situation appears to be more complicated than we allowed for. And before you ask, no, Captain; I can't explain it. I can only suggest that the walls have in some way become as infested with alien material as the Guardians. Which means the aliens have quite literally taken over the entire Base.'

'Those . . . creatures,' said Silence. 'Could they have been the aliens from the crashed ship? Some sort of hive mentality, perhaps? A group mind?'

Frost shrugged. 'It's possible, but unlikely. Given the size of the ship, I'd have to say the scale was all wrong. More likely the insects are tools used by the alien for some purpose. We have yet to encounter the real enemy.'

'Now there's a comforting thought,' said Carrion.

'Keep moving,' said Silence. 'We haven't even reached Level Two yet. Carrion; nice work with the lance. Stand ready; we might need you again.'

'Of course, Captain. It's nice to feel needed.'

'I could toss a grenade down ahead of us,' said Frost. 'If the aliens have any more surprises waiting for us down below, a shrapnel grenade should spoil their day quite thoroughly.'

'Nice thought, but no. The esper and the marines are still down there somewhere. Lead the way, Investigator.'

Their feet echoed hollowly on the metal steps as they continued down the stairway, the lamp hovering

benignly over their heads. Silence kept a careful watch
on the stairs and the walls, but there was no trace
anywhere of the vanished insects. Instead, a thick
viscous slime began to appear on the walls, oozing
down to coat the metal steps so that they became
treacherous underfoot. They slowed their pace,
taking it one step at a time. Thick drops fell from
somewhere high above, landing with sudden force
on heads and shoulders like heavy hands. The drips
fell more thickly as they neared the bottom of the
stairs, until it was a slow, unpleasant rain. Frost
stopped to wipe the stuff from her face, and found
she couldn't. The slime clung tenaciously to her
forehead, and flowed suddenly down to seal her eyes
and nose and mouth.

Silence and Carrion stopped with her as a thick
wave of slime rushed up the stairs and trapped their
feet and ankles in an unyielding grip. More rained
down from above, plastering their heads and faces.
Frost clawed at it with her hands, but it just oozed
between her fingers, leaving nothing for her to hold
on to. She kept her mouth firmly closed, and pinched
her nose shut. She didn't want the stuff invading her
body. There was already a growing pressure on her
closed eyes and in her ears. Silence tried to scrape
the slime from his legs with the edge of his sword,
but it just reformed around the blade without releas-
ing its hold for a moment. The goo was climbing his
legs like a slow rising tide.

And then it was torn from his legs and sprang away from his face and body, pulled away by an almost physical presence on the air. The slime also left Frost's face, leaving her gasping for breath. When more of it fell from above it couldn't touch them, pushed away and to one side by the presence. Silence looked at Carrion, who was frowning slightly, as though considering an interesting problem.

'Nicely done again, Carrion. You've improved your control since we last met.'

'I've had lots of time to practise,' said Carrion. A clear pathway opened up before them, forcing the slime off to the sides. 'We'd better make haste, Captain. I can't hold this stuff back for long; it's too diffuse. And the pressure's growing all the time.'

Frost and Silence clattered down the steps as quickly as they could, with Carrion crowding their heels. The slime rained down thickly, but couldn't get near them. A sudden wave rose up and threw itself at them from below, only to break and fall away to the sides as it met the pressure of Carrion's will. And then they reached the bottom of the stairs and moved quickly forward, leaving the slime behind them. Frost pulled a grenade from her bandolier and primed it.

'Incendiary,' she said briskly to Carrion. 'See how far you can get it up the stairwell before it explodes.'

Carrion nodded, and the grenade jumped out of Frost's hand and flew up into the gloom of the stairwell. There was a bright, vivid explosion, and crimson fire boiled down and outwards. The flames burned fiercely, but neither they nor the heat could get past Carrion's mental shield. The inferno leapt and blossomed, lighting the scene bright as day, consuming the slime hungrily. The flames died away bit by bit as the goo disappeared, until finally they were gone, and the quiet and the gloom returned. A harsh bitter smell filled the air, but nothing scuttled down the steps or oozed from the walls.

They looked about them, taking in the strange alien growths that sprouted from the metal walls and ceiling. Streamers of webbing hung down, twisting slowly back and forth, as though someone had just passed through them. Silvery traces glowed on the walls like living circuit patterns. And thick and heavy on the air, growing clearer by the moment, the stench of putrid meat.

'First insects that won't die, and vanish into solid walls, then living slime with homicidal tendencies, and now this,' said Frost. 'Whatever's hiding down here really doesn't want to be found.'

'Esper!' Silence's voice rang on the quiet, echoing faintly, but there was no reply. 'Stasiak, Ripper; where are you? Can you hear me? Diana?'

They waited, but the echoes died away with nothing to replace them. The shadows were still, and very dark, and deep enough to hide all kinds of secrets.

'Spread out and search this floor,' said Silence flatly. 'I want them found. Maintain contact at all times. And watch yourselves. Something down here doesn't like us at all.'

They moved apart and started the slow process of searching through the rubble and the deserted rooms and corridors. The continuing quiet was eerie and almost threatening, after the lengthy battles that had preceded it. There was a feeling of tension that grated on all their nerves. They found a huge hole in one wall, presumably made by a grenade or a Guardian, and several glowing holes that could only have been made by disrupters, but there was no sign of the esper or the marines, or of what they'd been fighting.

They finally returned to the foot of the stairwell, taking it in turns to look at each other and shrug and shake their heads.

'The Guardians must have taken them deeper into the Base,' said Frost finally. 'They could have been programmed to capture, rather than kill.'

'But Carrion told Diana how to handle them,' said Silence. 'They should have been easy targets for someone of her skills.'

'Something must have gone wrong,' said Carrion.

Silence nodded reluctantly. 'Find them, Carrion. Use your esp.'

The outlaw frowned, concentrating. Frost looked at Silence. 'I thought he was a polter,' she said quietly. 'Polters aren't normally telepaths as well.'

'There's nothing normal about Carrion,' said Silence, not bothering to lower his voice. 'The Ashrai saw to that.'

Carrion opened his eyes and breathed deeply, rotating his head as though to clear it. 'I can't find the marines anywhere. The esper is hiding in a clothes locker, just down that corridor. She's shielding herself, but I can feel her presence now I'm looking for it.'

'Why is she hiding?' said Silence.

'I don't know, Captain. But it feels like something bad has happened to her. Something really bad.'

He led the way down a side corridor, with Frost and Silence close behind, disrupters in their hands. Shadows loomed menacingly as the lamp floated along above their heads. Carrion finally stopped before a row of lockers, and looked at each of them thoughtfully. Silence looked at them disbelievingly. They were barely a foot and a half wide and six feet high, not even big enough to make a decent coffin. What could have frightened the esper so badly that she'd been driven to try and hide in such a cramped place? Carrion stopped before one locker, and tried the door. It wouldn't open. He frowned, and the door burst open, shattering the lock. Inside, Diana Vertue was half standing and half crouching, her arms wrapped around her, her eyes squeezed tightly shut. The posture would have been painful to hold for a few minutes; after all this time it should have been agonising, but she made no move to leave the locker. She showed no sign of even knowing they were there. Carrion reached out and gently touched her shoulder.

'She's gone deep inside herself,' said the outlaw quietly. 'Something happened here, something so awful she shut down her whole mind rather than think about it.'

'We need to know *what* happened,' said Silence. 'And where the marines are. Bring her out of it, Carrion.'

'There's nothing I can do, Captain. If I try and force her mind open, I could shatter it completely.'

'Then I'll have to do it,' said Silence. He knelt down beside the comatose esper, and laid a surprisingly gentle hand on her arm. 'Diana; this is Captain Silence. Please; wake up and talk to me. I need you to talk to me, Diana. Talk to your father.'

The esper stirred slowly. Carrion and Frost exchanged a quick glance of surprise, and then looked back at the esper as she slowly opened her eyes. She saw Silence kneeling beside her, and threw herself into his arms, sobbing loudly. He held her tightly and rocked back and forth, murmuring comforting words into her hair. He looked up, and saw Frost and Carrion studying him. He shrugged as best he could.

'They took her away from me when she was six. When her esp first started to manifest. I kept in touch as best I could, and when she graduated from the Academy, I got her transferred to my ship, where I could keep an eye on her. I thought she'd be safe, with me.'

Diana finally got herself back under control and stopped crying, sniffing back the last few tears. Silence let go of her, and helped her to her feet. She stretched awkwardly, wincing as cramped muscles protested.

'What happened, Diana?' said Silence. 'Why were you hiding? Did the Guardians take Ripper and Stasiak away?'

'I don't know,' she said, frowning. 'I can't remember. But it couldn't have been the Guardians. We beat them. Carrion showed me how. It was easy. And then . . . something went wrong, but I can't remember what.'

'Don't force it,' said Carrion. 'It'll come back to you.'

'There's only one place Ripper and Stasiak could have been taken,' said Frost. 'Down to Level Three. We're going to have to go down after them.'

'Yes,' said Silence. 'I think we are. Lead the way, Investigator. Diana; stay close.'

Frost glanced at him briefly, and then set off into the gloom with the esper close behind her. Silence and Carrion followed, hanging back a little.

'The esper really shouldn't be here,' said Carrion quietly. 'Whatever she saw, it frightened her so much she shut down her mind completely, rather than admit it happened. Her current mental state is precarious, to say the least. If she's forced to confront again the circumstances that caused her breakdown, her mind could fall apart. She could retreat so far into herself that not even the best esper shrink could bring her out again. Just making her stay here could be putting her under an impossible strain. Send her back to the pinnace, John. We don't need her here. You have me. My esp is more than strong enough to deal with whatever we find.'

'I need to know what she saw,' said Silence. 'Keeping her here will bring those memories back to the surface.'

'She's your daughter, John!'

'I'm Captain of the *Darkwind*. I know my duty.'

'Yes,' said Carrion. 'You always did. You haven't changed at all, John.'

He increased his pace to catch up with the two women. Silence looked at the three backs turned to him, and made no move to join them.

The stairwell leading down to Level Three seemed open and inviting. No insects crawled on the metal steps, and the walls were free of slime. There were still strange alien growths erupting from the walls and ceiling, and tattered webbing hung in thick grey coils, but the stairwell seemed untouched. Silence gestured for Frost to lead the way, and she started slowly down into the gloom, step by step, gun in hand. Carrion moved down after her, with Diana at his side. The esper's hands were trembling visibly, but her back was straight and she held her head high. Silence brought up the rear. He would have liked to be proud of his daughter's courage, but he couldn't afford to think of her that way. She was his ship's esper, and that had to come first.

The temperature rose sharply as they made their way down into the darkness, from bitter cold to almost suffocatingly humid heat. They turned off the heating elements in their uniforms, and pressed on in growing discomfort. The lamp still hung above them, buoyed up by Carrion's esp, but its light didn't travel far. They hadn't been able to find Diana's lamp, and she was unable to tell them what had become of it. She didn't speak much at all, but did as she was directed. She was an esper, and espers obeyed orders.

They reached the bottom of the stairwell without incident, and stopped a moment to get their breath. The heat was almost overpowering, and sweat dripped from their faces. All around them, the walls were cracked and pitted, and spotted with jagged outgrowths whose regular shapes suggested purpose, if not meaning. Stalactites of distorted metal hung down from the ceiling, dripping moisture that collected in pools on the uneven floor. The air was thick with the stench of rotting flowers.

'What the hell is this?' said Silence. He reached out and touched the nearest stalactite, and then snatched his hand away. The metal was painfully hot, the moisture almost boiling.

'This is something different,' said Frost. 'On Level Two the alien growths seemed wilder, almost out of control. This seems more pervasive, more planned. There's the same mixture of living and non-living materials, but the mix here seems more comfortable, almost organic.'

'But where did it all come from?' said Carrion, frowning. 'The aliens must have brought some of it from the ship, but there hasn't been enough time to bring about such extensive changes in the Base's structure. Besides; this doesn't look as though it was constructed; it looks more like it was grown this way.'

'Just like the alien ship,' said Frost, nodding. 'Whatever this stuff is, it isn't parasitic. There's a definite sense of purpose to it, of function. Symbiosis. Different systems working together, to reach the same end. This is an entire archology, taking over and supplanting the original one. The aliens' technology must be centuries ahead of ours, to have achieved so much so quickly. We have to get back to the pinnace, Captain. The Empire must be warned. Whatever's taken root here must be destroyed, down to the last fragment. If this should spread . . .'

Silence nodded. 'Odin; are you still in contact?'

'For the moment, Captain.' The AI's voice was quiet, but still clear. 'Audio contact remains firm. I am still unable to regain visual contact, and I have no contact at all with the missing marines. Something significant must have happened, either to the marines or their comm implants. I am maintaining a running log on this mission. In the event of my losing contact with you entirely, I will send a General Distress signal, and put this planet under full Quarantine.'

'Thank you,' said Silence dryly. 'Next time, you might wait for me to give the order. I am still in charge of this mission.'

'Of course, Captain. However, in order to present a complete log on this mission, I must have further data on the structural changes in Base Thirteen. To achieve this, it will be necessary for you to proceed further into the Base.'

'When this is all over, computer,' said Silence, 'you and I are going to have a long chat about which one of us is in charge, and you aren't going to enjoy it at all.' He looked at the others and tried not to scowl. 'Unfortunately, the machine's right. We do need more information, and the only way to get it is to press on.'

He stopped and looked at Diana, who was trembling violently. All the colour had dropped out of her face, and her eyes were very large. She realised he was watching, and made an attempt to stand straighter. She hugged herself tightly, and managed a shaky smile.

'I'm all right, Captain. Really. I've been trying to scan the area, but something down here is preventing me. I can't tell yet whether that's deliberate or not. I can't locate Ripper or Stasiak, but there are definite life signs all over the place. This whole Level feels like a jungle, but I can't focus enough to identify anything. The one thing I am sure of is that we're not alone down here. Something's watching us.'

'Can you be more specific?' said Silence, careful to keep his voice cool and unconcerned. He didn't want the esper any more upset than she already was.

Diana bit her lip and shook her head. 'Something's down here, Captain. I don't know what or where it is. But it knows we're here.'

She stopped suddenly, as though she'd been about to add more, and then changed her mind. Silence waited a moment, but it was clear the esper had said all she was going to. She still looked scared, but she was back under control again. For the moment.

'All right,' he said briskly, 'we're going in. If anything moves, kill it. We don't have any friends down here.'

'What about the marines?' said Carrion.

'The odds are they're dead,' said Silence flatly. 'Otherwise Diana or the computer would be able to locate them. We'll search for them as we go, but they can't be our main objective. We're looking for the aliens. Anything else has to come second.'

'Of course,' said Carrion. 'People always come second, as far as the Empire's concerned. When in doubt, shoot first and ask questions later. If at all.'

Frost shrugged easily. 'We go with what works. Now let's get a move on. I don't like us standing around like this. It makes us too good a target.'

She started off down the corridor, stepping carefully over the uneven floor, and the others followed her. The heat grew steadily heavier and more oppressive as they moved deeper in, and condensation fell from the ceiling like intermittent rain. Alien growths blossomed on the walls, complex and enigmatic. Great fleshy petals uncurled from outgrowths of bone spliced with metal, and huge structures of living clockwork moved steadily towards some unknown goal. Some shapes seemed to border on the edge of purpose and meaning, but still evaded human understanding.

At one point the corridor became choked with a thick mass of the grey webbing, and they had to stop and cut their way through with their swords. It was slow, back-breaking progress as the sticky mesh tore reluctantly under the blades. Sometimes Silence thought he saw strange lights flashing briefly in the darkness, but the others never mentioned them, so he kept his peace till he could be sure himself. The esper began to frown heavily, and stopped at times to stare intently at some new outgrowth or alien structure.

'She's starting to remember,' Carrion murmured to Silence. 'I'll keep an eye on her.'

And then they rounded a corner, and Diana

stopped dead and screamed. Carrion and Frost moved quickly forward to stand between her and what she was looking at. She managed to swallow the second scream, but she was trembling so violently she could barely stand. Silence moved in beside her, and had to fight down an urge to look away. They'd finally discovered what had happened to the missing personnel of Base Thirteen.

Stretched across the wall, interspersed with alien growths and mechanisms, were recognisably human shapes and organs. Bodies had been torn apart and reassembled in strange patterns. Alien technology mixed with brightly veined meat, and nerves and wires curled around familiar bones. And every organ and stretch of tissue was still clearly alive and functioning, as part of a new, monstrous whole. Stasiak's face peered blindly from a shifting spider's web of silvery traces. There were no eyes in the face, but a muscle twitched regularly by the slack mouth.

'It's alive,' said Carrion quietly. 'I can feel it in my mind. It shouldn't be alive, but it is.'

'Just like the alien ship,' said Frost. 'Living and non-living tissue cyborged together. A biomechanical gestalt whose whole is greater than the sum of its parts. This is functioning, Captain; it has a purpose, a reason for existence.'

Silence looked at Diana. Her mouth was slack, and her eyes saw nothing at all. He looked back at the living wall. 'At least now we know what happened to

the marines. They must have been taken and ...
broken down, in front of Diana. No wonder she
blocked out the memory.' He looked at Diana again,
and then away. The empty eyes were more accusing
than any stare could have been. 'Why didn't they take
her, too?'

'Espers have a unique defence mechanism,' said
Carrion coldly. 'In times of danger, they can use their
esp to become psionically invisible. Can't be seen or
heard. You could walk right into one and not notice.
Apparently it works equally well on aliens, too. You
can ask Diana all about it, when she wakes up. If she
wakes up.'

'If she can't keep up with us, we'll have to leave
her behind,' said Frost.

'I know,' said Silence. 'I know.'

They walked along the wall, trying to take in the
details. Carrion took Diana by the hand and she
walked along beside him, her face completely blank.
The lamp still hovered above them, its pitiless light
revealing every awful detail of the living surface. Half
a brain bulged wet and glistening from a silver and
grey latticework, next to a pale bloodless hand whose
fingers curled and uncurled, over and over again. A
single eyeball gleamed dully among copper piping
beaded with sweat. An endless display of viscera
wound back and forth, intertwined with gold and
silver wiring. Frost studied it all with cool fascination.

Silence couldn't look away. Carrion mostly looked after Diana, who went where she was led.

There were more walls, equally disturbing, and as the party moved deeper into Level Three, the mix of living tissue and alien technology became increasingly overt and bizarre. One hundred and twenty-seven men and women had lived and worked in Base Thirteen, before the aliens came, and not one part of them had been allowed to go to waste.

'Why?' said Frost finally. 'What's the point of it all? What is this supposed to achieve? If the aliens were capable of such extensive work, why didn't they use the Base's . . . resources to repair their ship?'

'Perhaps the ship was too badly damaged,' said Carrion. 'Or perhaps this . . . construction was the reason the aliens came here. We need more information, and a context to see it in. For the moment, we're just guessing.'

'We need to find the aliens,' said Silence. 'They can't be allowed to get away with this.'

'Captain,' said Odin quietly in his ear, 'I have been examining the memory crystal discovered on the crashed alien vessel, and I have finally managed to access the information within. I have arranged it in as palatable a form as possible. I strongly suggest that you study it now.'

'All right,' said Silence. 'Run it for me first, then run it for Carrion and the Investigator, while I stand watch. Be prepared to break off at a moment's notice, if necessary.'

'Of course, Captain. Stand by.'

Silence's vision shimmered, and was suddenly replaced by strange alien vistas as the AI patched the memory crystal directly into his comm implant.

Tall towers, draped in strands of glass and pearl, under a mercury sky. Silvered clouds boil slowly around a sun too bright to look at. The towers stand alone on an endless plain. There are dim cavities in the sides that might be entrances. Something living curls around the bases of the towers, unfurling wide jagged petals to the brilliant sun. The images are blurred, seen through a fluid, distorting haze.

A series of similar images come and go, where the details change but the scene remains the same. The towers age but do not fall, the strands twisting and shuddering as time shakes them. More towers spring up, covering the plain. In and out of the cavities, around the bases of the towers, near and far, are shadowy figures, never still, always blurs. It is as though frames from a film, taken some time apart, have been laid side by side to give an illusion of movement.

Something is speaking, though not with words. Information is passed, thick with meaning.

The towers are everywhere, linked by bridges of gossamer webbing. Life is everywhere, leaping, soaring, growing. There is no room. Time passes. There is war among the towers. Fire burns and terrible energies blaze. The dead are everywhere. Life is everywhere.

A line of shapes, huge and metallic, each different from the next, appear on the plain. They throw themselves up into the mercury sky, and are gone.

Silence rocked on his feet as the images left his sight, and would have fallen if Frost hadn't steadied him. He leaned on her a moment, till his legs steadied, and then nodded to the Investigator that he was all right. He waited a moment while Odin ran the alien memories through Carrion and Frost's minds, and then they looked at each other with new eyes.

'Incredible,' said Frost. 'A species, a civilisation, where the boundaries between animate and inanimate, living and non-living, have been blurred and forgotten. Everything there was alive, struggling for space and survival.'

'No room anywhere, any more,' said Carrion. 'So they built or grew starships and set off to find new worlds. New planets to conquer, to infest, to make over in their image. That's what's happening here. The Base has been remade into something more . . . familiar.'

'More than that,' said Frost. 'Base Thirteen is a beacon, calling others of its kind. They have to be stopped, here on the Rim, while they're still confined to one world. If this were to spread . . . The Empire must be warned. The aliens must be destroyed.'

'Not aliens,' said Silence. 'Just the one. Each of those ships carried a single creature. Or rather, each of those ships was a single creature. Our visitor left its shell after the ship crashed, and made a new shell for itself here, in Base Thirteen. We have to find it, and kill it. If we can. I'm not sure if it is life, as we understand it.'

'We can't take chances,' said Frost. 'Not with something like this. Our very species is at risk. Our best bet is to return to the Darkwind and use atomics on the Base until nothing's left but a few grains of dust, glowing in the dark.'

Silence looked at Carrion, who nodded slowly. 'We'll have to find the force-shield generator and shut down the Screen first.'

'Are you hearing all this, Odin?' said Silence. 'How are your repairs going? Can you be ready to take off once we've shut down the Screen?'

'I'm sorry, Captain,' said the AI, 'but I can't take you anywhere. You have all been exposed to the alien organism. The probability is high that you are yourselves infected. I cannot risk you passing on that infection to the Darkwind.'

'Odin, this is a direct order from your Captain,' said Silence. 'Stand by to carry us back up to the Darkwind, where we can be kept in Quarantine . . .'

'I'm sorry, Captain. My standing orders override

yours. You will remain here. The pinnace is barred to you.'

Carrion laughed softly. 'Isn't that the bottom of the line with the Empire, John? Everyone's expendable. Everyone.'

CHAPTER NINE

Unexpected Complications

Silence fell helplessly through darkness without end. The bitter air was thick with the stench of sulphur and burning blood. Bright lights flared about him, flashing past like blazing comets. There were voices in the dark, loud and meaningless, interspersed with screams and laughter. Silence didn't know how long he'd been falling, but it felt like for ever. He thrashed about him, hands searching frantically for something that might slow his fall, but there was only the dark and the cold wind rushing past him. He forced himself to stay calm, his mind racing. Where was he, and how the hell had he got there? Where were the others? Where was Carrion?

'Right here, Captain.'

And suddenly he was standing on a narrow stairway, its cracked marble steps falling away into infinity. Carrion stood beside him, calm and unruffled. The cold wind stirred his hair, and his cloak swirled around him like billowing wings. He looked down at the endless drop, and then looked at Silence, unmoved.

'I did warn you, Captain. A trip like this is always dangerous.'

'Trip?' said Silence, his voice harsh to hide the uncertainty. 'Where are we, Carrion?'

'Where you insisted I take you. Inside Diana Vertue's mind.'

Memories returned in a rush. Diana had seen the marines die, ripped apart before her. Horror and survivor's guilt had overwhelmed her mind, until the only way to save her sanity had been to deny it had ever happened. She forgot it all, until she was forced to remember. And then, rather than face the horror again, she'd shut herself away inside her own mind, where nothing could reach her and nothing could harm her. She shut herself down, and stood staring blindly, mute and comatose, safe at last.

Carrion couldn't reach her with his esp, but he did have one suggestion. It was risky and uncertain, dangerous both to him and the esper, but he could drop his shields and join his mind directly with Diana's. Make her pain his own. *If you're going in there, I'm going in with you,* Silence had said. *After all, I am her father.* Carrion had argued, and Silence hadn't listened. He had no choice. He needed the esper if he was to complete this mission successfully. And she was his daughter, after all.

Lights blazed in the darkness, guttered and were gone. Voices came and went, shrill and inhuman. And the wind, blowing out of nowhere.

'Every light is a thought,' said Carrion softly. 'Every voice a memory. The rising and falling of the wind, the force of her will. We're a part of her mind now, as vulnerable as she is. Either we find a remedy for her madness, a way for her to live with her memories, or we'll never leave here.'

'Where did the stairway come from?' said Silence, as much for the comfort of hearing his own voice as anything else.

'It's a construct created by our joined minds; a symbol of constancy, to help us feel more secure. You must expect strange things here, Captain. The mind deals in symbols. Particularly when dealing with things it doesn't really want to think about.'

He looked down, and Silence followed his gaze. The stairway ended not far below in a shimmering silvery plain that stretched away in all directions further than the eye could follow. And there, at the foot of the stairs, a great white-walled house with strange lights burning in its windows.

'That is Diana's consciousness,' said the outlaw. 'Or how she perceives it. We have to enter the house and put right the damage there, if we can. We'd do well to make haste. Time isn't a factor; a few days here can be only a few seconds in the real world. But the mind is a dangerous place to visit. All the things we really fear are here, with nothing to protect us from them save the strength of our own wills. There are no rules here, Captain; only varying degrees of necessity.'

'Then let's get on with it,' said Silence, and he started down the stairs towards the great white walls.

The house drew slowly closer, as though reluctant to accept any visitors. Silence began to get the feeling there was something else in the darkness with them. He looked unobtrusively about him, but the dark turned aside his gaze with contemptuous ease. He heard slow, regular breathing, and what might have been the flapping of giant wings. The sounds came first from one side and then the other, growing steadily closer, nearer. Silence could almost feel a hot, arid presence, watching from the concealing darkness.

'Ignore it, Captain,' said Carrion softly. 'Whatever it is, we don't want to meet it. Concentrate on the house. Just the house.'

And suddenly they were at the foot of the stairway, the house looming over them, shining like a moon. The great structure looked old-fashioned and strangely stylised, as though built more for viewing than actual use. The strange lights were gone, and the windows held only darkness, like so many watching eyes. A sudden chill stabbed through Silence as he finally recognised what he was looking at. It was the doll's house he'd bought Diana for her fifth birthday. When she'd still been his child, before the Empire took her from him. He looked at the door before him. It was a great featureless slab of wood, without knocker or handle.

'What do we do now?' said Silence. His voice seemed to echo on and on, falling away into disturbing whispers.

'We go in,' said Carrion evenly. 'And then we talk to Diana, or whatever part of her she chooses to show us. We can't force her to come back with us. We have to persuade her. If we can.'

He stepped forward and knocked firmly on the door. The sound was flat and empty, not at all like a door should sound. It swung slowly open before them, revealing a brightly lit hallway. Silence looked at Carrion, who gestured for him to lead the way. Silence stepped resolutely forward, Carrion a step behind. The door closed behind them with a solid, final sound. The hallway stretched away ahead of them, impossibly long. The light came from everywhere and nowhere, and doors led off at regular intervals.

'The mind is a labyrinth,' said Carrion. 'Let's hope we don't meet the Minotaur.'

'There might not be one,' said Silence.

'There's always a Minotaur. If we're lucky, there'll also be a guide.'

As though the house had been listening all along, and waiting for the word to be spoken, a door opened not far away, and a young child stepped out into the hallway. Diana, six years old, in her party dress. There were electrode burns on her forehead.

'Do you recognise the image, John?' said Carrion. 'Do you know why she chose this of all her selves to show us? This is what she looked like when the Empire was training her to use her esp. Or to be more exact, when not to. The first thing all espers have to learn is obedience; only to use their esp when ordered. Espers are controlled through pain-avoidance conditioning; a long and painful process whose only justification is that it works. No one uses the word "torture". Espers have no rights. They're a commodity, to be used and discarded as needed. And if that means attaching electrodes to a young child and turning up the voltage, well, you can't make an omelette, and all that. No, Captain; don't look away. This is your doing.'

'I didn't know,' said Silence.

'You didn't want to know. You closed your eyes to evidence, and your mind to rumours, and told your-self it was all for the best. You sent your daughter to Hell, John, and part of her is always there, endlessly suffering, endlessly screaming. And we're going to have to walk through it to reach her.' Carrion leaned forward, his voice gentle as he spoke to the child before him. 'Diana; we need to talk to you. Can you speak to us?'

The child turned, put out her hands for them to take, and led them down the hallway. The small hand was warm and soft and very real in Silence's grasp. Ghosts came and walked in the hall with them, pale and silent people who'd been important to Diana in her short life. Silence didn't recognise any of them.

There was no sign of himself among the ghosts. They filed past in eerie silence, their eyes preoccupied, their thoughts somewhere else. Some of them bore the brands of the electrodes on their skin. Some were screaming soundlessly, some were clearly insane, and too many of them were children.

Silence looked away, studying the doors they passed. Some were closed and some were open. The rooms held moments from Diana's past, endlessly repeating like flies trapped in amber. Most were scenes of suffering, mental or physical and often both. *You sent your daughter to Hell, John.* Silence wanted to look away, but wouldn't let himself. And then they came to a closed door, behind which a small child sobbed endlessly, without comfort or hope, and Silence stopped. Carrion and the child stopped with him. Silence stared at the door, his hands clenched unknowingly into fists, and it seemed to him that if he opened that door and stepped through, he could save his daughter and undo the evil that had been done to her. Carrion looked at him sharply, and there was something in the outlaw's eyes that might have been fear.

'There's nothing you can do, John. What you're hearing is the past. It's already happened. In some deep part of our mind, everything that ever hurt or scared us is still there, waiting for a chance to attach itself to us again. If you open that door, and let loose what's in that room, you condemn Diana to Hell again, and us with her. Come away, John. The odds are you'll have to face worse than this before we reach the core mentality; the deep hidden centre of Diana, the self that never sleeps.'

'We shouldn't be here,' said Silence. 'This is more than just an invasion of privacy. There are things no one should have to see or remember.'

'You're right,' said Carrion. 'But we don't have any choice. Diana's gone too deep into herself to find her way out again without help. I'm not even sure I can get us out of here without Diana's co-operation. If I try it alone, I could destroy her mind, or worse. I told you all this before we came here. It's a bit late to be getting an attack of scruples.'

'She's my daughter, Sean.'

'No, John. You gave up any claim on her, when you handed her over to the Empire mind-techs. We have to go on, John. We have to go deeper.'

Silence nodded stiffly, and allowed his daughter and the man who used to be his friend to lead him on down the hall. Ghosts swirled around them, lost in the past, and there were doors beyond number. Silence came to another one that was closed, from behind which came screams of hate and fury. Something huge and powerful slammed against the door, rattling it in its frame. The thick wood cracked and splintered, but still held. Diana pulled insistently at Silence's arm.

Silence allowed her to pull him away from the door, and they continued on their way. The light grew gradually dimmer, and the floor no longer seemed as solid under his feet as it once had. And then, out of the darkness, Ripper and Stasiak came striding forward, leaving bloody footprints behind them. Silence stepped to one side to let them pass, but they stopped before him, blocking the way. They stared at Silence, and tears of blood ran down from their unblinking eyes.

'Why did you do it, Captain?' Stasiak whispered. 'Why did you bring us down here and then abandon us? Please, Captain; I want to go home. Don't leave me here in the dark.'

'They're just images,' said Carrion. 'Your mind gives them strength. They can't harm us, unless you let them.'

'Please, Captain,' said Ripper. 'Don't leave us here.'

'Whatever happens,' said Silence steadily, 'I swear I won't leave you in Base Thirteen. One way or another, I promise I'll set you free.'

He walked forward, with Carrion and Diana, and the marines stepped aside to let them pass. Doors came and went, and ghosts walked, but finally the hall ended in a single huge doorway. The child Diana let go of Silence and Carrion's hands, produced a large brass key from somewhere, and unlocked the door. She pushed it open easily, despite its apparent weight, and gestured for Silence and Carrion to enter. They did so cautiously, and found themselves in a small cosy room with comfortable furniture, and a small fire crackling pleasantly in an open hearth. Diana, her rightful age again, sat at her ease in one of the chairs by the fire. Silence looked slowly about him, frowning. The child was gone. The door shut quietly behind them.

'I know this place,' said Silence. 'I remember this. Elaine and I brought Diana here when she was very small. It was our last holiday together.'

'Probably why she chose this memory out of them all to hide herself in,' said Carrion. 'She felt safe here. The last place she ever felt safe and protected from the outside world.'

They looked at Diana in the large, over-stuffed chair. *It wasn't really that big*, realised Silence. *She just remembers it that way because she was so small.* Outside, he could hear rain falling. It had rained all through that holiday, and he and Elaine and Diana spent the long days playing games and charades, and stuffing themselves with good food. Not much of a memory to make a heaven out of. But when it's all you've got . . .

'Diana,' he said finally. 'It's me. Your father. I've come to fetch you. It's time to go.'

'I don't want to go,' said Diana. 'There's something out there. In the dark. It frightens me.'

'You can't stay here,' said Carrion. 'The longer you stay, the harder you'll find it to leave.'

'I don't want to leave,' said Diana. 'I'm safe here.'

Something moved outside the shuttered windows.

Footsteps, slow and steady, passing by, heading for the door.

'Who's out there, Diana?' said Carrion.

'My mother. She was here too.'

All the colour dropped out of Silence's face as a cold hand clutched at his heart. 'No, Diana. No! Your mother's been dead five years now.'

'Not here,' said Diana. 'You were here and I was here, and Mother was with us. We're all going to be together, and we'll never have to be alone again.'

The footsteps reached the door, and stopped. There was a feeling of anticipation, of something final and irrevocable about to happen.

'The door's locked,' said Carrion. 'Concentrate, John. The door is locked if you believe it to be. John; listen to me. She mustn't be allowed to complete the memory, or we could be trapped here with her.'

'Elaine,' said Silence. 'You never met her, Sean. You would have liked her. She was bright and funny and very lovely. She died in an attack ship ambush, out by the Horsehead Nebula. They never found the body, but we held a funeral for her anyway. I miss her, Sean. I miss her so much.'

The handle of the closed door rattled. Silence looked at it and then back at Diana. Carrion clutched his arm tightly.

'John, Diana; don't do this. The more real you allow your past to become, the more power it has over you. You're in control now, but it won't last.

Everything that ever made an impression on you, for good or bad, is in here with you. For the moment, all the things that frightened and hurt you are safely locked away behind closed doors, but once you lose control, the doors will start opening. And then, it won't be Elaine rattling the handle and wanting to come in. John, talk to her, damnit. Convince her. You said yourself that Elaine's been dead for five years. What do you think is out there? At best, you're faced with an eternity of child's games and charades. At worst, you're facing an eternity with a woman you know is dead.'

Silence looked at the door, and then at Diana. She smiled at him serenely.

'Diana; we can't stay here. You have to come with me now.'

'No. We're going to be together again. For ever and ever and ever.'

'Diana . . .'

'Something happened,' said Diana. 'I don't remember what, and I don't want to. I'd rather die than remember.'

'No!' said Silence. 'Diana, please; listen to me. We need you. I need you. I've been alone so long . . . I've got to go. Please; don't leave me alone again.'

She looked at him steadily. No sound came from beyond the door. It felt as though the whole world was holding its breath. Diana reached out and took Silence by the hand.

'Look after me,' she said quietly. 'Keep me safe. Promise.'

'I promise,' said Silence, forcing the words past an obstruction in his throat. 'I'll never let anything hurt you again.' He took her in his arms, and she hugged him tightly, her face buried in his chest. Silence looked at Carrion, his eyes bright with unshed tears. 'Get us out of here, Sean.'

A blinding light filled the room, washing away every detail in its glow. Then it faded and they were back in the corridor on Level Three. Back in another labyrinth, with a different Minotaur, held together by newly discovered love. Carrion hoped it would be enough.

'All right,' said Silence. 'This is the plan. It's very simple. Simple plans are always the best, because that way there are less things to go wrong. Diana; you're going to use your esp to contact the alien. The thing itself, the beast in the shell; whatever it was that first came here from the crashed ship. You're going to act as bait, to draw the alien out from wherever it's hidden. It'll come to you, because it perceives you as a threat. Your esp makes you especially dangerous, and it knows that. You don't have anything to worry about; Investigator Frost will be with you. She'll keep both of you alive, and the alien distracted while Carrion and I track down the heart of the system it's built here. There has to be a centre, a place that holds everything together. Destroy that and the alien will be isolated, and much more vulnerable to attack.

'Carrion will use his psionic invisibility to keep the alien from knowing what's happening till it's too late. Once we've broken the connection between the alien and the Base, Frost should have no trouble in dealing with it. But Diana; you must understand that once we've started this, we have to finish it. You can't disappear behind your psionic invisibility, and hide; you're the bait. You have to hold its attention while Carrion and I destroy the heart. You'll be in no real danger. Frost will protect you.'

'Damn right,' said the Investigator. 'Never met an alien I didn't kill.'

Diana nodded jerkily. 'I understand, Captain. Let's do it.'

She closed her eyes and let her mind drift up and out. The Base roared around her in a thousand voices, some human, some not. The human components of the alien system were still alive, though their minds or what was left of them now followed alien paths. Diana concentrated on blocking out the babbling voices one by one, searching for the dominating alien presence at the centre of its web. It found her first, blazing in her thoughts, but she held her ground and kept the alien firmly at the edges of her mind. She felt its interest in her grow as she continued to hold it at bay, and its thoughts crawled across her shields like worms across her face. Its probes grew stronger and more threatening, but Diana had been trained to withstand far worse.

Her confidence firmed as she realised the alien wasn't really that strong in itself; its true strength lay in the shell it had built around itself, in its domination of the living components of its web. Diana shut out every other voice, concentrating on the alien, showing it her strength. Its thoughts seethed at the edges of her mind, dark and complex and utterly inhuman. Try as she might, its thought processes made no sense at all. Diana concentrated on projecting a single message; *If you want me, you're going to have to come and get me yourself. Your web can't see me, and if you don't come to me, I'll come to you. And I'll destroy you.* The alien broke contact sharply, and Diana dropped back into her head and opened her eyes. The others looked at her questioningly, and she nodded firmly; trying hard to look professional and in command of the situation.

'It knows where I am. You'd better get moving, Captain. It'll be here soon.'

Silence smiled and nodded. 'Just give me a direction, Diana.'

Diana projected the map overlay the AI had given them of Level Three, and indicated their position and that of the centre of the web. Silence and Carrion acknowledged the information, and Diana broke contact. Silence waited patiently while Diana familiarised herself with the new lamp the Investigator had found, and then he and Carrion set off down the corridor, their lamp bobbing along above them like an over-sized will-o'-the-wisp. Diana and Frost stood together a moment, awkward in each other's company, and then the Investigator sat down on the floor, drew her sword and laid it across her knees.

'Might as well make ourselves comfortable, while we wait for the alien to put in an appearance. I take it your esp will give us plenty of warning?'

'Of course, Investigator.' Diana hesitated, and then sat down beside Frost. It didn't feel particularly comfortable, but it was good to get off her feet for a while. 'So, what do we do now, Investigator? Just wait?'

'Pretty much. Nothing we can do till the alien gets here. Relax. Save your strength. You're going to need it.'

'What do you suppose it'll look like?' said Diana hesitantly. 'I've never seen an alien. In the flesh, as it were.'

'Could be anything,' said Frost easily. 'None of this fits in with anything I've ever seen before. Probably really ugly. Most of them are, to our eyes. Don't let it worry you. As soon as it shows up, I'll blow a hole through it with my disrupter, and then you can help me cut it up into bite-sized pieces. No problem.'

'How can you be so calm, so confident?' said Diana. 'This creature slaughtered every living thing in the Base, and then tore their corpses apart to fashion them into a living computer network. This isn't some rogue animal we're dealing with; it's a powerful, sophisticated entity, and it's heading right for us.'

'I'm an Investigator,' said Frost. 'I'm trained to deal with situations like this. Are you scared, Diana?'

'Yes,' said the esper. 'Yes, I am.'

'That's good. Being scared will give you an edge. It gets the adrenalin pumping, and sharpens your reflexes.'

'Are you scared?'

'I suppose so, in my way. Investigators don't really have emotions, just pale echoes of what we remember emotions being. Our training sees to that.'

Diana nodded. 'Training. The usual Empire euphemism for mind control. They started my training when I was six years old. When to use my power, and when not to. Who to use it for. And right from the beginning it was made clear to us that if we didn't learn thoroughly or quickly enough, we'd be killed. The Empire won't tolerate rogue or uncontrollable espers. Six years old is a hell of a time to be made aware of your own mortality. But it does give you a strong sense of perspective. In the end, all that really matters is following orders.

'They experimented for a time with mind-control implants, but they couldn't develop one that didn't interfere with esper functions, so they settled for good old-fashioned psychological conditioning. I've been trained about as thoroughly as anyone can be, without an actual lobotomy.'

There was a pause as they sat quietly together, not looking at each other.

'My training started at about the same age,' said Frost slowly. 'In learning to out-think alien minds, we give up a lot of what it means to be human. Things like emotions, conscience, companionship. Our training produces warriors; perfect killing machines to serve the glory of the Empire. I don't feel much of anything any more, except when I'm fighting. I've had lovers, but I never loved any of them. I have no friends, no family, nothing but the job. Still, if nothing else, it is an extremely interesting job.'

'Is that all you have?' said Diana. 'Just the job and the killing?'

Frost shrugged. 'It's enough. You can't expect too much out of life, esper. You should know that.'

Diana smiled briefly. 'You know, we're more alike than I thought. You deal in death and I deal with life, but really we're two sides of the same coin. We both had our childhoods taken away from us, and had our lives shaped into something those children could never have understood. And we'll both probably die serving the same people who destroyed our lives in the first place.'

Frost shook her head. 'No, esper; you don't understand me at all. I like being what I am, what they made me. I'm strong and I'm fast, and there's nothing and no one that can stand against me. I'm the most perfect fighting machine you'll ever see. I've been

responsible for the destruction of whole alien civilis-
ations, and killed men and creatures with my bare
hands. It's only when I'm fighting and killing that I
feel really alive. It's like a drug you never grow tired
of. You can't know how it feels, esper; to know
you're the best. I'm the ultimate expression of the
Empire; the personification of its strength and purpose. And all I had to give up to achieve it was a few
weak emotions that would only have got in the way
anyway.

'It's different for you. You take no pride in being
an esper. Probably give it up tomorrow, if you could.
To be normal. I won't give up what I am, and I'll kill
anyone who tries to take it away from me. You think
too much, esper. It gets in the way. Life's so much
simpler without conscience or emotions to compli-
cate things.'

Diana looked at her steadily. 'Everything else has
been taken away from me; I won't give them up too.
I'd rather die.'

'You may get your chance,' said Frost, looking
down the corridor into the darkness. 'Something's
coming.'

The Investigator rose to her feet in one graceful
movement and stood listening to the quiet, sword at
the ready. Diana scrambled inelegantly to her feet and
looked wildly about her. The alien couldn't be here
already. It couldn't. Her esp would have picked it up
long before this. Unless it too knew the art of psionic

invisibility. In which case, things were about to get rather interesting.

Frost slapped the metal bracelet on her left wrist, and her force shield sprang into existence on her left arm; a palely glowing rectangle of pure energy, humming loudly in the quiet. Diana raised her esp and reached out tentatively. The Base was silent, with none of the babbling voices she'd heard earlier. The alien had put up shields. Diana retreated quickly into her own mind, and set up her own wards. Theoretically, they should be able to stand off any psionic attack, up to and including a mindbomb, but she'd never tested her shields in actual conflict before. She hoped the alien didn't know that. She glanced across at Frost, and was quietly reassured by the Investigator's obvious professionalism and competence. A thought struck her.

'Investigator; if the alien is coming, wouldn't you be better off with your disrupter than your sword?'

'No,' said Frost calmly. 'A sword's more versatile. You can have the gun, if you want.'

'No thanks,' said Diana. 'I don't believe in them.'

'Suit yourself,' said Frost, a shrug clear in her voice. 'Whatever's out there, it's close. I can feel it. I'm impressed. I didn't think anything could get that close without me knowing.'

'Psionic invisibility,' said Diana. 'No way you could have known.'

'That shouldn't have made any difference,' said

Frost. 'I am an Investigator, after all. Are you picking up anything?'

'Not much. Something's coming, and it's not alone. I don't think it's the alien.' She looked unhappily at Frost. 'I can't be sure, but I don't think the alien's here at all. It's still hanging back. It's sent something else in its place. Stand ready, Frost. They're almost here.'

'Relax, esper.' The Investigator swept her sword casually back and forth before her, smiling easily. 'Nothing's going to get to you while I'm here. Though you could at least activate your force shield. There's no point in making it easy for them. You're here as bait, not a sacrifice.'

Diana blushed, and slapped her bracelet. The low hum of the force shield was very reassuring. She and the Investigator stood quietly together, listening. And then the soft patter of running feet came clearly to them out of the darkness, and Diana and Frost braced themselves as their enemy finally emerged into the light.

They'd been human once, before the alien absorbed them into its system. Now they were something else, roughly human in shape, but refashioned to meet the alien's needs. They were crooked and malformed, the flesh had run and congealed on their frames like wax melting on a candle. Some had no skin, the red muscles shining wetly in the lamplight, their tendons twitching with every movement.

Bunches of cilia waved from empty eye sockets and mouths held needle teeth. Muscles bulged impossibly, beyond restraint or reason. The twisted faces were inhumanly blank, indifferent to thought or emotion. The alien had reworked them for its own reasons, and if there was any humanity left in them, it was buried deep, where it wouldn't interfere.

There were ten of them, jostling together at the edge of the lamplight, as though reluctant to leave the comfort of the shadows. *Ten*, thought Diana. *That's not so bad. We can handle ten.* As if in answer to her thoughts more appeared, stepping out of the steel walls as though they were intangible as mists. The Investigator scowled.

'How do they do that? Those walls are solid. I checked them myself.'

'The walls have become part of the alien system,' said Diana quietly. 'They're as alien as everything else in this Base now. The whole structure has become a single great organism, with the alien as its heart and mind.'

Frost snorted. 'So what does that make these things?'

'Antibodies. We're invaders, an infection in the system. So those things are going to cleanse us out.'

'You mean they're going to try,' said Frost calmly. 'All right, there's a lot of them, but they're not even armed. Let's keep this in perspective, esper. We can handle this.'

'You don't get it, do you?' said Diana. 'They're *antibodies*. The alien can make as many of them as it needs to, recycling damaged ones if necessary. It can make a dozen, a hundred, a thousand; as many as it needs to overrun us. Even you couldn't stand against a thousand, Investigator. They're not human. Not any more. They don't think or feel or hurt. They'll just keep coming until we're dead. And then the alien will recycle us, and put us to some useful task. If we're lucky, we'll never know what.'

'You think too much, esper,' said Frost. 'It's never over till it's *over*. With this many antibodies, they'll spend most of their time tripping over each other and getting in each other's way. All we've got to do is hold them off, until either the Captain and the outlaw reach the heart of the system, or the alien gets impatient and comes here itself to take us on.' She smiled unpleasantly at the shapes before her, and swept her blade back and forth. 'Come on then, you useless sons-of-bitches. Let's do it.'

Captain Silence and the outlaw Carrion moved swiftly through the distorted corridors, heading into the dark heart of Base Thirteen. For a long time the only light came from the lamp bobbing along above them, but eventually strange lights began to appear in the distance, steady glows and sudden glares, like the opening of so many watching eyes. Things stirred and shifted in the shadows, sometimes alive and sometimes not. Silence kept a wary eye on all of them, but tried not to look at them too closely. Something about their uncertain shapes disturbed him on some deep, primal level. The idea that the material world could acquire sentience and direction undermined his faith in how the universe worked.

Carrion, on the other hand, didn't seem to be bothered by any of it. But then, he'd been an Investigator once, and nothing bothered them. Silence glared about him, holding his gun so tightly that his knuckles ached. He had faith in Carrion's psionic invisibility to keep them from being detected, but walking straight into the alien's clutches went against everything his instincts were telling him. He clamped down hard on his nerves, and watched where he stepped. Thick steel cables stirred sluggishly on the floor like dreaming snakes, coiling around each other in slow, sinuous movements, dripping black oil. Silvery traces glowed like veins in the sweating walls, pulsing to a fast, irregular rhythm. Silence glanced at Carrion, irritated by his continued calm.

'Are you sure this invisibility of yours is working?'

'Quite sure, Captain. Because if it wasn't, we'd very likely be dead by now. Have faith, Captain. I'll get you there.'

Silence sniffed. 'Odin; are you still following this?'

'Yes, Captain,' the AI murmured in his ear. 'Audio contact remains firm.'

'Give me an overlay of the Level Three floor plans.'

The plans appeared before him, hovering on the air in glowing lines and symbols. Silence checked his position and that of the centre of the web, and scowled. They were a lot closer than he'd thought. 'Odin; any chance you've reconsidered your position on letting us back on board the pinnace?'

'No, Captain. My Security imperatives are very clear on the matter. However, I will of course provide you with whatever information and guidance I can.'

'Any more useful information from the Base computers?'

'Not as yet, Captain. However, there are still several areas locked away behind Security codes I don't have access to.'

'All right; lose the overlay.' The glowing map vanished from his sight. 'Stay in contact, computer. Let me know of any changes in the situation.'

'Of course, Captain.'

Silence looked at Carrion. 'I take it you were patched into that. Any comments?'

'Only that we should walk very carefully from now on. We're nearly there, and I can't believe the alien will have left the heart of its system unprotected. There are bound to be defensive systems and booby traps just waiting for us to trigger them.'

'I've really missed your sunny personality, Carrion. You look for the worst in everything, don't you?'

'Yes, Captain. And usually, I'm right.'

Silence sniffed. 'We should reach the heart in a few

minutes. Assuming we do find a way past whatever's waiting for us, do you have any ideas as to what we're going to do when we get there?'

'Not really, Captain. A few of your grenades, backed up if necessary by a channelled psi-storm from me should be enough to wreck whatever the alien's put together, but I can't be sure until I've seen it.'

'Aren't you going to make a speech about how wrong I am to be planning the destruction of a new alien species? I seem to recall you were quite eloquent on the subject where the Ashrai were concerned.'

'That was different. The Ashrai were willing to co-exist. This species is not. Its existence is based on total restructuring and control of the environment. They are as much a threat to this world and the Ashrai as they are to the Empire.'

'I wish you'd stop talking about the Ashrai as though they were still alive. They're dead and gone. I killed them all. You've been alone here too long, Carrion.'

Carrion looked at him almost pityingly. 'The Ashrai aren't gone. You never did understand the bond between the Ashrai and the metallic forest. I've been here ten years, and I'm only just beginning to comprehend what we destroyed here. The Ashrai were a race of espers, exhibiting psi phenomena we could barely measure, let alone understand. They fought the Empire to a standstill, for all our superior tech-

nology. And even though you scorched this planet,
they're still here. Their bodies may be dead, but their
souls still haunt the trees. Call it a vast living field of
psi energy and phenomena earthed by the metal
forest, if that makes it easier for you to grasp. But as
long as the forest still stands, the Ashrai still exist.
They do not forget and they do not forgive. They
were very special, John. You never did understand
what you did here.'

'Oh yes, Sean. I know what I did.'

Carrion stopped suddenly, and gestured for Silence
to stop with him. They stood a while in their narrow
pool of light, while Carrion frowned uncertainly,
checking the way ahead with his esp. He finally shook
his head and gestured for Silence to continue, but he
was still frowning. Silence drew his gun and scowled
at every moving shadow. The pressure of unseen
watching eyes seemed heavier by the minute, but
nothing challenged them.

The corridor widened out suddenly into what had
been one of the main computer bays, and Carrion
and Silence stopped again, halted by the sight of what
lay before them. The machines had burst apart from
pressure within, and flowered into unsettling half-
living constructs, held together by long glistening
strands of human nervous tissue. A low constant
muttering filled the air, so quiet as to be almost
subliminal, as the hybrid creations worked constantly
on unknown alien tasks. Silence looked slowly

around him, not allowing himself to be hurried, no matter how much the sight revolted him. Carrion walked slowly forward, his face blank, his eyes fey and knowing.

'This is the heart of the system, the centre of the web,' he said quietly. 'Through this, the alien controls all that happens in the Base. This is its eyes and ears, its brain and memory. Destroy this, and the alien will be cut off from its creation. The Base systems will fall apart, and the alien will be left alone and vulnerable.'

'If it's that straightforward, what are you looking so unhappy about?' said Silence.

'It's too easy. Too easy to get here and too easy to destroy. It can't be this simple. We must be missing something. I think we should investigate these systems very carefully before we do anything else.'

'Carrion; we don't have the time. The alien's gone for the moment, but it could be back any minute. We have to destroy the heart while we can. Look, just because the alien is intelligent and powerful, it doesn't necessarily follow that it's very bright. The more powerful an organism, the less it needs to think things through. It uses what has always worked in the past, and expects that to be enough. Because it's never been beaten, it thinks it can't be. Everything has a weak spot, and we've found the alien's. Now give me some room and let me work. Watch the corridor if you want to be useful. I want to set the grenades and get the hell out of here before the alien realises something is up and comes charging back.'

The outlaw nodded stiffly, and moved away to watch the corridor, still frowning. Silence consulted with the AI, and worked out the best places to set his grenades to ensure maximum damage. He planted three grenades carefully, primed them all one after the other, and then sprinted back down the corridor with Carrion at his side. They'd just rounded the first corner when the first grenade blew. A shockwave of super-heated air laced with jagged shrapnel came howling down the corridor, to slam harmlessly against the psychokinetic shield Carrion set up. Two more explosions followed in swift succession, and the floor trembled under their feet. The explosions were deafeningly loud, and Silence clapped his hands to his ears, grinning triumphantly. Smoke filled the corridor, billowing, thickly around them. The tremors finally died away, and the corridor was quiet, save for the crackling of distant fires. Silence grinned at Carrion.

'That should ruin the alien's day nicely. You'd better run a scan, though; just in case any of that stuff is still working. I'll have the AI check it out from its end.'

He broke off as the AI's voice suddenly sounded in his ear. 'We have a problem, Captain. Apparently Base Commander Starblood wasn't content to just seal off the Base with a force Screen, he also activated the

Base's self-destruct system. A small nuclear device
was primed and programmed to detonate at the end
of a countdown. When the alien's systems took over
the computers, it interrupted the countdown, but
didn't defuse the bomb. As long as the system was in
control, the countdown was unable to continue, and
the Base was safe. Now that you have destroyed the
alien system, the countdown is proceeding again. The
nuclear device will detonate in thirty-two minutes,
and I do not have the necessary codes to abort it. I
strongly suggest that you leave the Base now. While
you still can.'

CHAPTER TEN

Friendships and Loyalties

Frost pulled a concussion grenade from her bandolier, primed it, and lobbed it casually over the heads
of the watching humanoids. A few turned their blank
faces to follow it, but the others showed no reaction,
even as Frost primed and threw two more grenades.
The first exploded deafeningly in the midst of the
humanoids, blowing a bloody hole in their ranks.
Smoke filled the corridor, and blood flew on the air
in a crimson mist. The next two grenades blew
seconds later, while Frost and Diana huddled back
into a niche in the corridor wall, hands clapped to
their ears. The massed ranks of the humanoids
absorbed the force of the explosions, scattering blood
and mangled bodies the length of the corridor. The
living and the injured staggered aimlessly back and
forth, dazed and confused, and Frost chuckled easily
as she shot the head off a humanoid with her disrupter. Diana shrank back from the open violence in the
Investigator's voice, and brushed furiously at the
blood that had spattered her clothes.

The humanoids milled back and forth, clawing at

the smoke and each other. Frost laughed softly,
hefted her claymore and moved forward with a light,
easy step. Her blade flashed in the lamplight as she
cut and hacked her way through the blank-faced
drones. Her sword jarred on bone and sliced through
flesh, and she was everywhere at once, darting back
and forth. Bodies fell to either side of her and did not
rise again, and the humanoids reached blindly out
into the smoke and chaos as the alien will behind
them struggled to orientate itself. Investigator Frost
cut and hacked a path into the heart of the enemy,
and was content.

Diana Vertue concentrated on maintaining her
psionic invisibility, balancing her need for safety with
her duty as bait. She allowed a vague sense of her
presence to leak through her mental shields, to keep
the alien's attention, but hid her precise location
behind a screen of ambiguity, so that neither the alien
nor its humanoid slaves could tell exactly where she
was. They milled around her with reaching hands, a
horrid faceless mass of clawed hands and snapping
mouths, but none of them could find her, even when
their bodies bumped into hers. She bit down hard on
her lower lip to keep from screaming. The humanoids had been constructed from the Base personnel,
and though they moved and fought and searched
with stubborn purpose, they were still dead. Their
faces held no thought or emotion, their skin was
deathly cold to the touch, and something strange and

alien looked out from their unblinking eyes. Diana stood with her back pressed tightly against the wall, her face contorted with a horror beyond revulsion, shrinking away from every contact. A slow grinding headache built in her left temple, sharp-edged and blinding, as she struggled to maintain the delicate balance of her presence. There but not there. Present but not seen. And over and above everything else, the certain knowledge that if her control slipped, even for a moment, the humanoids would turn on her and tear her apart.

Frost danced and strutted in the midst of her enemies, pirouetting with sharp professionalism, her sword swinging in unstoppable arcs. It was a good blade, Old Earth steel, and whilst it might not have the edge of her monofilament knife, the weight and power of the claymore was more than a match for the clawing hands of the alien drones. They swarmed about her, a living sea of hate and violence, and none of them were fast enough or good enough to touch her. Their clawed hands snatched and tore but she was never there, defying them to find or hold her. Her force shield brushed aside the few humanoids who got too close, the glowing energy field fending off their unnatural strength. But its constant use was a dangerous drain on its energy crystal, and it wouldn't be long now before the shield collapsed. Frost didn't care. The humanoids were falling before her, and she was in her element, doing what she was trained and born to do. Nothing could stand against her. Let them come. Let them all come. She was an Investigator, humanity's warrior, and the alien was going to learn what that meant.

Diana watched the Investigator butcher the dead men from Base Thirteen with grace and style, and it seemed to her that Frost was as inhuman as what she was fighting. The Investigator's face was a cold mask of contempt and professionalism, with no trace of compassion or cruelty. She killed because that was what she'd been trained to do, and because she was good at it. An expert in the art of slaughter. Not that Diana had much compassion herself for the humanoids. She could see in their faces that they weren't human any longer in anything but shape. Death was the only peace and dignity they could attain to. She supposed she should be helping Frost fight, but she couldn't. Partly because the effort to maintain her invisibility took so much out of her, but mostly because just the thought of violence on her part sickened her. The Empire had trained her well.

And then, suddenly, the humanoids fell back, turned away from the Investigator, and disappeared into the surrounding steel walls. One moment the corridor was full of smoke and baleful figures, and then they were gone, and the smoke was slowly clearing to reveal Frost lowering her bloody sword in puzzlement. She wasn't even breathing hard. The dead lay where they had fallen, jagged metal showing in bloody wounds, and gore still spattered the floor and walls, but Frost and Diana were alone in the corridor. Frost sniffed disappointedly and moved back to stand with Diana, shaking drops of blood from her blade. The esper shrank back from the gore-soaked sword, but Frost didn't notice. She clapped Diana on the shoulder, and looked around her with an easy and contented smile.

'It looks like we were too much for them. Pity. I was just starting to enjoy myself.'

'It's not over,' said Diana softly. 'Something's coming.'

The Investigator looked at her sharply, and then glared about her, sword at the ready. 'Is it the alien?'

'It must be. It burns in my mind like a beacon, wild and brilliant. It hurts to think about it. There's something . . . wrong about it.'

'How close is it?'

'Close. I can hear it thinking. It doesn't make any sense. It has emotions, but I don't recognise any of them. It's like seeing new colours in a rainbow . . .'

'You're wandering, esper,' said Frost. 'Keep to the subject. How big is the alien? How strong? Which direction is it coming from?'

'It's almost here.' Diana rubbed at her forehead as her headache flared up again. 'It's getting harder to keep it out of my mind. It's like looking into the sun when it's too bright . . . It's strong, powerful. Inhumanly powerful.'

'Concentrate, esper.'

'I can't . . . there's too much of it . . .'

'Then bring it here. Be the bait, and I'll take care of everything else.'

And then the alien appeared at the end of the corridor, and Frost stopped talking. It was big, filling the corridor from wall to wall and from floor to ceiling, like a slug in its tunnel. The dark ribbed body looked long and powerful, with thick cables of muscle standing out and pulsing like veins. Metallic strands threaded through its flesh, not added, but a living part of its body. Long bony limbs protruded at regular intervals along its bulk, poling it along the walls. Sharp metal barbs and spikes thrust up from its glistening back, and its tail was too far away to be seen. The blunt head had no eyes, or any other obvious features, but metallic teeth snapped shut again and again in its wide maw, like the closing of a mantrap. The mouth was big enough to take a human head as a morsel, and the teeth shone like daggers. It surged forward, foot by foot, huge and threatening like a thunder cloud come down to earth. Its limbs rattled against the metal walls, and breath hissed in the vast mouth.

Diana wanted to look away, but couldn't. On some deep, basic level the thing offended her. It was a mixture of living and unliving, life and technology, but grown, not made. Things that should never have known sentience or animation were an intrinsic part of its being. She tried to imagine what kind of hellish pressures or evolution could produce such a creature, and couldn't. It was too alien, too different. The creature blazed in her mind, the strength of its presence blasting aside her shields till she stood naked and helpless before it. The alien looked at her with its blind head and knew where she was, and the shape and texture of its thoughts were made clear to her. They made no sense to her, no sense at all.

'It's bigger than I thought,' said Frost casually. 'It must have grown considerably since it left its ship, presumably from feeding on the Base personnel. I wonder how big it would grow eventually, without restraint . . . Still, that's a problem for those that come after us. Stand back, esper. I'm going to blow a hole right through it.'

'Your gun won't stop it,' said Diana. 'Nothing can stop it. It's too big. Too different.'

'Hell,' said Frost. 'It's just an alien.'

She raised her disrupter, trained it on the alien's blunt head, and pressed the stud. The searing energy bolt burned a hole through the head, and black oily blood spattered across the walls and ceiling. The alien howled deafeningly, the sound reverberating through Diana's bones as much as her ears. Its head swayed back and forth, and Frost looked on dumbly as the ruptured flesh knitted itself together again, steel and silver traces scabbing over the gaping wound like metal sutures. Frost put away her gun.

'I think we're in trouble, esper. I was rather count-
ing on the disrupter to take care of the alien. Still,
when a plan fails, improvise. I've got a few grenades
left. When I say the word, you run. And don't hang
about, because I'm going to be right behind you.'

She pulled a grenade from her bandolier, hefted it
casually, and then primed it and rolled it along the
floor towards the alien. She yelled to Diana, and the
esper turned and fled down the corridor. The alien
lunged forward, its bulk smothering the grenade.
Frost turned and ran, quickly catching up with the
esper. Frost hurried her on with harsh words, and
then saved her breath for running. The grenade went
off, and the floor shuddered under their feet. Frost
allowed herself a moment of satisfaction, until the
alien's voice filled the corridor, harsh and unrelent-
ing. The floor trembled again, this time from the
massive weight that bore down on them in pursuit.
Frost tried to visualise how fast something that big
could move, but had to abandon the thought.
Nothing in her training or experience had prepared
her for this alien. It was too different, too unlike
anything humanity had ever encountered before.

She accessed the floor plan, and led Diana into the
smaller, narrower corridors, hoping they'd prove too
small for the alien's bulk. But everywhere they went,
the alien had been there first. Strange growths
erupted from the sweating steel walls, and shimmering strands hung down from the torn ceiling. And

finally they had to stop for Diana to get her breath back. Frost looked impatiently around her while the esper leaned on her arm for support, head hanging down as she fought for air. The Investigator was still breathing slow and easy. Her training had prepared her for worse than this. She could have escaped the alien easily if it hadn't been for Diana, but she couldn't bring herself to abandon the esper. As long as the bait was still held dangling before the alien, it should concentrate on the esper and not concern itself with what Carrion and the Captain were doing.

She glared back down the corridor into the impenetrable gloom, gun in one hand, incendiary grenade in the other. She might not be able to kill the alien, but she could sure as hell hold its attention. She looked unhurriedly about her, sizing the corridor up for possible ambushes and hurried exits. There were holes everywhere, in the walls and in the ceiling, some of them leading into tunnels apparently big enough to swallow the *Darkwind*'s pinnace. The alien had been busy.

Frost frowned suddenly as she realised the trembling in the floor had stopped. The alien must have decided on another route, a roundabout way to take its prey by surprise. Which meant any of the holes might become an opening for the alien's attack. She approached the nearest of the larger holes and peered cautiously down it. Deep in the darkness she heard a faint muttering, a familiar cacophony of human and alien voices. She primed the incendiary grenade, counted three quickly, and threw the grenade as far down the tunnel as she could, before stepping to one side and flattening herself against the corridor wall.

There was a dull roar, and smoke and flames billowed out of the hole, along with flying fragments of alien tissues. Frost grinned savagely, and then trotted down the corridor with Diana in tow, pausing to scorch each of the larger holes with a blast from her disrupter. The vivid energy bolts lit up each tunnel as she fired, but there was never a trace of the alien, and the gun took a little longer each time to recharge between shots.

Frost stopped near the end of the corridor, and peered uncertainly about her. She was doing a lot of damage to the Base, but she was no nearer stopping the alien. It should have found them by now. She wasn't foolish enough to think they'd lost it, or left it behind, which meant it had to be planning something in its devious, inhuman mind. Frost smiled. In her own quiet way she was enjoying the chase. It was the first real challenge of her abilities she'd ever had, the first opportunity to try and out-think something that didn't think the way humanity did. She had the upper hand. As long as she and the bait kept moving, the alien was helpless to do anything but chase her. It was too large, too heavy, and too stupid to do anything but follow where she led. And when the Captain and the outlaw had destroyed the heart of its web, she'd turn on the alien and have it run for a while, while she pursued. She snapped her head round suddenly as she caught a faint whisper of the alien's muttering again. She looked at the esper, who was standing with her eyes closed, trembling violently.

'It's here,' said Diana. 'It's found us.'

'Where is it?' said Frost. 'I can't see it anywhere.'

'Close,' said Diana. 'Close.'

Frost looked quickly back and forth, straining her ears for any more of the alien muttering, but nothing moved in the corridor gloom, and the air was still and silent. Frost frowned, and tapped her gun against her thigh. Wherever it was, she should still get plenty of warning of its approach. The alien couldn't get anywhere near them without the floor trembling underfoot to alert them. Even if it came through one of the tunnels in the walls. And then something made her look up.

The blunt head emerged from a vast hole in the ceiling like a maggot in a rotten apple. Frost grabbed Diana and hurled them both frantically to one side as the alien dropped out of the ceiling and the floor shuddered. Frost hit the ground rolling and was quickly back on her feet again, a grenade in her hand. She primed it, rolled it down the corridor towards the alien, hauled Diana upright and all but threw her round the nearest corner. She counted quickly under her breath as they ran down the side corridor, and

then a blast of superheated air blew past the corridor
entrance, followed by the alien's roar. Frost grinned.
She might not be able to kill the damn thing, but she
could still hurt it.

She pushed the esper ahead of her as they ran, and
took the opportunity to examine her disrupter. The
energy crystal was seriously depleted, good for only
three or four shots at most. The floor was trembling
again. The alien had to be close behind them. She
risked a look back, and swore dispassionately. It was
nearer than she'd expected, and getting nearer. The
thing could move surprisingly fast for its bulk. Frost
smiled briefly. She'd always been the pursuer before,
never the pursued. This was a new experience for
her. She found it exhilarating.

They rounded the next corner and then skidded to
a halt as they found the corridor was a dead end.
According to the floor plan, it should have been an
open passage, but the alien had sealed it off some
time earlier with a thick mass of webbing. Frost
hefted her disrupter. The gun still had enough power
to blast a way through, but she might need it yet.
Frost shrugged, and levelled the gun at the webbing.
The vivid energy bolt tore through the web, blacken-
ing the ruptured edges. Frost started forward, only to
stop as the web slowly reformed, knitting itself
together with effortless skill. The way was blocked
again, and she'd wasted one shot. She didn't see any
point in wasting another. She looked quickly about

her. There were more of the holes in the walls and ceiling, and no way to tell where any of them led. The alien had been busy. Frost turned to the esper, who was looking back the way they'd come with wide eyes and trembling mouth.

'We're going to have to make a stand, esper. Or rather, I am. You can't help me, and you might get hurt if you got in the way, so I want you to go on alone. Pick one of the tunnels. They have to lead somewhere. Choose one of the smaller ones and the alien won't be able to follow you. I have to stay here and hold its attention until the Captain and Carrion have finished their business.'

'You can't face that thing on your own,' said Diana. 'The gun didn't hurt it, and the grenades only slowed it down. If you stay here you'll be killed. Come with me. I'll make us both invisible, and we'll lose the alien in the tunnels.'

'No, esper. We have a job to do, remember? We have to keep the alien occupied.'

'You can't do that if you get yourself killed. Stay here and you'll die!'

Frost raised an eyebrow. 'It's not that certain. I am an Investigator, after all. We can't both go into the tunnels. They're unknown territory to us. Certainly the alien has to know their layout a damn sight better than us. You go on, esper. I'll hold it here. You have to survive, to be the bait again, if necessary. And if you're going to lead the alien a chase without me, you're going to need a good head start. Go on, esper.'

Diana looked at her steadily. 'You're going to die here, aren't you?'

'Not if I can help it.'

'Aren't you?'

Frost sighed resignedly. 'Yes, esper. Quite probably. But that doesn't matter. I know my duty. I always knew I'd die in the field and not in my bed. Comes with the job. I don't mind. It's my duty and it's my life. It's all I've ever wanted.'

'You mean it's what the Empire made you want. They programmed you, just like they did me. They ruined your life and made you love it, and now you'll die for them, because your conditioning won't let you do the sensible thing and run.'

'No, Diana; that's not it. I'm going to stand and fight because that's what I do best. We're buying time for the others, me by fighting, you by running. Now do as you're told and get into that tunnel. Please.'

Diana stepped forward suddenly, and hugged Frost tightly. The Investigator just stood there for a moment, and then gently hugged her back. Diana let go, and Frost helped her climb into the nearest tunnel mouth. Diana smiled back at Frost, her lips pressed tightly together so they wouldn't tremble and spoil the moment, and then she turned and disappeared into the tunnel, taking her lamp with her. Frost adjusted her eyes to make the most of the ambient light, and turned back to face the corridor. Her force shield hummed briskly on her arm, and her sword was a comforting weight in her hand. She breathed slowly, coolly, and her hands were perfectly steady. What the hell. It was only an alien. Something moved in the shadows at the end of the corridor, and Frost smiled widely.

At the heart of the alien web, Carrion and Captain Silence looked at each other speechlessly as the AI told them of the nuclear countdown in a calm, conversational voice. Silence slammed his gun back into his holster.

'Well that's great. Just great! Now what the hell are we going to do?'

'If I might suggest, Captain,' said Carrion, 'this is something we might do better to discuss on the run. We have less than thirty-two minutes to locate the esper and the Investigator, evade the alien, get the hell out of Base Thirteen, persuade your computer to let us back on the pinnace, and get off planet before the nuke blows.'

'In other words,' said Silence, 'we're going to die. What the hell; we might as well give it a try, just to be awkward. Odin; work out where we are and show us the quickest route out of here.'

'I'm afraid I can't do that,' said the AI. 'Firstly, I will not let you back on board the pinnace. You are still quite probably contaminated by the alien. Secondly, the Empire is going to need the alien's body, and as much of its technology as possible, to examine. Given the potential threat of this new species, the Empire will need all possible information as to the extent of that threat. I must insist you do all in your power to preserve the Base and its contents. I regret the necessity for such harsh measures, Captain. My programming requires that I do this. You know how it is.'

'Just when you think things couldn't possibly get any worse, they do,' said Silence. 'I'll make you a deal, Odin. You agree to get us off planet and safely back to Quarantine on the *Darkwind*, and we'll save the Base and its contents from destruction. What do you say?'

'Agreed,' said the AI. 'My programming allows me to be flexible during emergencies.'

'Right,' said Silence. 'That's a start, anyway.'

'Pardon me,' said Carrion. 'But just how are you planning to defeat the alien and defuse the nuke in under thirty-one minutes?'

'Beats the hell out of me. Odin; you must have forged some links with the Base computers by now; can't you patch into the systems running the countdown, and turn it off?'

'Not at present, Captain. Since this was intended as a last-ditch self-destruct option, the Empire built in a great many safeguards to ensure that the countdown could not be interfered with, once initiated. The alien managed to suspend the countdown in some manner, but I confess I am at a loss to explain how. I am doing my best to access the relevant systems, but my best-guess analysis suggests that will take me significantly longer than the thirty-one minutes remaining on the countdown.'

'Didn't you just know he was going to say that?' Silence said to Carrion. 'Do you have any ideas?'

'Do we know where the bomb itself is located?' said Carrion, frowning thoughtfully.

'Well, computer?'

'The exact location is protected by Security codes I do not have access to. Logic suggests it is concealed somewhere on Level Three, to ensure maximum destruction.'

'Whatever we're going to do, we'd better do it quickly,' said Carrion. 'And we have to contact Frost and Diana. They may be facing the alien by now, and they still think they have all the time in the world to deal with it.'

'There is a way,' said Silence slowly. 'After all, this doesn't affect just us. We're not alone on this planet, are we, Carrion? There's always the Ashrai.'

The alien came boiling down the corridor towards Frost like a flash flood, impossibly huge, impossibly fast. Its mouth gaped wide, revealing teeth like knives. It was on the Investigator in a second, and she launched herself forward, vaulting over the alien's lowered head and on to its spiked metal back. She landed awkwardly, trying to dodge the spikes and the barbs, but quickly regained her balance. She swept her force shield round in a circle, the sputtering edge shearing through the spikes, and then, having made herself some room, she slammed her sword down into the alien's head. The blade sank half its length into the leathery flesh, and the alien howled shrilly. It smashed its head against the corridor wall, trying to shake off the pain it felt, but Frost held on to the sword with both hands, and kept her balance.

Thick black blood pooled around her feet, and Frost grinned savagely as she stirred the sword around in the alien's skull, searching for the brain. The alien screamed, the vast sound hammering through Frost's head, and its long body convulsed as it struggled to throw her off. Frost used all her strength and forced the sword in another few inches. She worked the blade from side to side, trying to widen the wound, but even as the dark flesh split apart metal traceries sprang out of the raw meat to repair the damage. The flesh healed incredibly quickly, and the metal sutures were strong enough to resist her sword's edge. And slowly, inch by inch, the sword was being forced back up and out of the wound it had made.

Frost lifted the force shield on her arm and brought it down like a hammer. The edge of the energy field passed through the leathery flesh like mist, leaving a long rent behind it. She knelt down beside her sword, and the force field spat and sparkled as she buried it in the alien's back. The alien threw itself back and forth, its wailing voice painfully loud as its cries echoed and re-echoed back from the corridor walls. Frost fought back as it whipped its head from side to side. Metal spikes thrust up around her, and her shield jerked out of the alien's back. She leaned on her sword with all her strength, but still the blade was forced up and out of the alien flesh.

And then a pit opened up in the alien's back beneath Frost's feet, and sucked her down. She was knee deep in the alien before she could even react, hidden muscles crushing her legs. She snarled at the pain and cut desperately about her with her sword and her force shield, but still the alien flesh sucked her down. It closed around her like a living sea, absorbing her struggles and repairing its wounds as fast as Frost could make them. She groped for the monofilament knife in its sheath on her leg, but it had already disappeared into the alien's body. Something dragged at her feet, pulling her down till she was waist deep in the alien. The dark flesh rose up like a tidal wave and swept towards her.

Diana looked down from the mouth of a tunnel high up on the wall, and clenched her fists helplessly as she watched the Investigator disappearing into the alien's back. She knew she should be using the time Frost was buying her to get away, but she couldn't just turn her back and let the Investigator die. She

couldn't just leave her. A cold hand clutched at her
heart as the tidal wave rose up and rolled unstoppably
forward. Unless she did something, and quickly,
Frost was going to die. But what could she do? She
was an esper, not a fighter. Never a fighter. She looked
wildly about her for inspiration, and her gaze stumbled across a massive, blocky wall unit not far from
the tunnel mouth.

She didn't stop to think about what she was going
to do, because she knew that if she did, she probably
wouldn't do it. First, she had to get the alien's
attention. She dropped her mental shields and cast
aside her invisibility like a veil she no longer needed.
The great alien head swung round immediately,
staring up at her blindly but knowingly. It wanted
her, and now it knew where she was. Frost was still
sinking into its back, but more slowly now, as though
it wasn't concentrating on her any more. It had her,
but it wanted the esper. The huge body surged
forward, its stumpy legs poling it along the walls,
leaving dents in the steel in its wake. Diana slapped
the bracelet on her left wrist, and her force shield
sprang into being on her left arm. The alien lifted its
head high, searching for her. Diana leaned out from
the tunnel mouth, hanging precariously by one hand,
and cut at the wall unit with the edge of her shield.
The shimmering energy sliced through the unit's
supports, and it lurched drunkenly away from the
wall, held only by a single cable. She leaned out

further, most of her weight hanging out over the drop. The alien's head reached for her, only inches away. Diana gritted her teeth, stretched out her arm, and sliced through the remaining cable. The unit tore itself away from the wall and crashed down, its massive weight hammering the alien's head to the floor.

Diana dropped on to the alien's back, aiming carefully to land between the trapped Investigator and the pinned-down head. She hacked at the dark flesh with the edge of her shield, until Frost could get her arms free again, and then between them they dug the Investigator out. The alien thrashed back and forth, convulsing down all its length, unable to get enough leverage to lift its head against the weight of the wall unit. Frost finally got her hand on her monofilament knife, and together with Diana she cut herself free. They climbed quickly down from the alien and backed away down the corridor, both of them spattered with gore.

'Do you think that weight's going to hold it?' yelled Diana, shouting to be heard over the din of the alien's howls.

'Not a chance!' yelled Frost. 'Let's get out of here.'

She ran down the corridor with Diana at her side. Behind them they heard a crash as the alien finally threw off the wall unit. Diana tried to run faster, and couldn't. Her strength was gone, and she was running now on desperation and adrenalin. The Investigator ran effortlessly beside her, not even breathing hard, even after all she'd been through. It occurred to Diana that Frost could probably get away quite easily, but instead had chosen to run at the slower pace. She looked round suddenly and caught the Investigator's eye.

'You didn't have to save me,' Frost said brusquely. 'You could have got away.'

'I know that.'

'Then why did you do it? Why risk your life to save mine?'

'Because you needed me,' said Diana. 'Now shut up and run.'

'What about the invisibility? Any chance . . .'

'No. Not now the alien's locked on to me.' She looked back over her shoulder. The alien was flowing down the corridor after them, faster than they were running, faster than they could run. Diana looked at Frost. 'Don't ask. You don't want to know. Just run.'

Silence's voice was suddenly in their ears, murmuring through their comm implants. 'Investigator, esper; we've destroyed the heart of the alien's web. It is now completely cut off from the rest of the Base. Have you located the alien yet?'

'Oh yes,' said Frost. 'We know exactly where it is.'

'Good. Do you think you could lead it to where Carrion and I are at the moment? We've had an idea.'

The floor plan of Level Three flashed briefly before Frost and Diana's eyes, showing them the route.

Diana thought hard. It wasn't far. They might just make it. She looked at Frost, and nodded briefly.

'We can be there in four minutes,' said Frost calmly.

'Make it three,' said Silence. 'We're working to a rather urgent deadline. Bring the alien here, and we'll discuss what to do next. Silence out.'

'The Captain's got a plan,' panted Diana.

'Yes. Interesting he didn't tell us what it was. Probably because he knows we wouldn't like it.' She looked at Diana. 'Can you last three minutes at this pace?'

'Shut up and keep running,' said Diana.

'Are you sure you want me to do this?' said Carrion. 'Once I call up the Ashrai, there'll be no turning back. I don't think you realise just how much they hate you.'

'They'll hate the alien more,' said Silence. 'That creature and its kind threaten the existence of the whole planet. They wouldn't just destroy the forest, they'd change it into something the Ashrai wouldn't even recognise. And since the Ashrai depend on the forest for what's left of their existence, it's in their interest to side with us against the alien.'

'Very logical, Captain,' said Carrion. 'I just hope the Ashrai are going to be logical too.'

'The enemy of my enemy is my friend. Nothing like having something in common to bring two peoples together.'

'You still don't understand, Captain. Once I summon up the Ashrai, they pass beyond my control. Once woken, they might decide not to lie down again. You didn't really win here, John. You just hurt them so badly they retreated back inside themselves for a time. There's power here on Unseeli, power beyond your worst nightmares. They might decide to take on the Empire again. And this time they'd have nothing left to lose; nothing to hold them back.'

Silence shook his head. 'So? You're talking about billions of people on thousands of worlds. The Ashrai wouldn't stand a chance.'

'John, you're talking about numbers. I'm talking about power.'

'It doesn't make any difference,' said Silence. 'We don't have any choice. Too many things have gone wrong, and we've too many strikes against us. Frost and the esper will be here any minute, with the alien right behind them. We've run out of options, Sean. Odin; how does the countdown stand?'

'Nineteen minutes, thirty-two seconds, Captain.'

Silence looked at Carrion. 'Get yourself ready, Sean. We'll do it as soon as the others arrive.'

They both looked round at the sound of running footsteps, and Frost and Diana came pounding down the corridor towards them. Silence looked past them, but the corridor behind them was empty. Diana staggered to a halt, gasping painfully for air. Frost supported her with one hand as she nodded calmly to Silence. She wasn't even breathing hard.

'The alien's right behind us, Captain. It slowed down a bit when it realised where we were going, but it's still mad enough to keep after us, once it's looked around for a trap. I take it there is a trap here, Captain?'

'Oh yes,' said Silence. 'Have you hurt it at all?'

'I shot it and blew it up with grenades, and Diana dropped half a wall on it, but all we did was annoy it.' She looked round at the destruction of the alien's heart, and raised an eyebrow. 'Very thorough, Captain. You do realise that everything here will repair itself, given enough time?'

'Time is something we're all rather short of, Investigator. Before he died, Commander Starblood found time to activate the Base's self-destruct system. A small nuclear device hidden somewhere on this Level is due to detonate in just over eighteen minutes.'

Frost looked at him. 'You're jinxed, Captain; you know that?'

Diana raised her head and glared at him speechlessly, still too out of breath to talk, but her eyes spoke volumes.

'Whatever you're planning, Captain; start it now,' said Frost. 'The alien will be here any second, and it's in a really bad mood.'

'Don't look at me,' said Silence. 'It's all down to Carrion now.'

'Yes,' said the outlaw quietly. 'Somehow, it always comes down to me.'

'Because you're the best, Carrion.'

'Thank you, Captain.'

Diana wiped the sweat from her face with her sleeve, and then raised her head suddenly. 'Listen. It's close now. Very close.'

They all looked down the corridor, into the gloom. There wasn't a sound to be heard, but they could all feel a faint vibration in the floor under their feet. Silence looked at Carrion.

'Please, Sean. For them, if not for me.'

Carrion smiled slightly. 'You always did know how to fight dirty, John.'

Silence nodded, and moved away to stare down the corridor. Frost joined him, and they trained their disrupters on the concealing shadows. Diana finally straightened up as she got her second wind, and found herself a corner to stand in where she could be out of everyone's way. Carrion stood alone in the centre of the room, leaning on his staff, his thoughts elsewhere. He couldn't help feeling he'd come a long way by strange routes to reach this place, this moment. Everything he'd been through, all the rage and fear and heartbreak, just to end up fighting beside John Silence once again. Carrion smiled slightly. Whatever happened, it was good to have seen John again. It was like finding an old coat you used to wear, or a cup you used to drink from when younger.

Comforting in its familiarity, tested in its worth, something you could depend on. Silence was back, at his side, and if he had to die this was not a bad way to go, among people he liked and respected.

Among people. It had been a long ten years, without a human face or a human voice. But still, there had been the Ashrai.

He lifted up his legs and sat cross-legged in mid air, hovering alone in the middle of the room, his staff lying across his knees. He reached deep inside himself and unlocked his power, channelling it through his power lance, calling up everything he'd ever been or hoped to be. He could feel his esp building, pressing at his shields, eager to be free and loose in the world. He had learned many things in his time on Unseeli, whether he'd wanted to or not, walked paths few humans even knew of, and it had changed him. He was more than human now, a bastard child of Man and Ashrai, and the alien was about to find out what that meant.

He threw his mind up and out, searching for the voices in the wind that were always there, just on the edge of his consciousness. Bright lights blazed, dazzling him with their presence. They were old and powerful and utterly inhuman, warm and familiar and comforting; his friends and his adopted people. He called, and they came for him, where they would not have come for any other. The outlaw Carrion, once a man named Sean, talked to the Ashrai in a language and manner that had nothing human in it.

Silence looked back at Carrion, floating unsupported in mid air, and felt his hackles stir uneasily. There was more than ten years' difference in the outlaw's cool, serene face, and sometimes it seemed to him that he didn't know this man Carrion at all. His voice was still the same, but sometimes Silence thought he saw someone else looking out at him through Carrion's eyes. Silence shrugged mentally. He'd put all their lives in that familiar stranger's hands, and it was too late now for second thoughts. His head snapped back as something stirred in the darkness at the end of the corridor, and then the alien came storming out of the shadows towards them, horribly fast and unstoppable. It raised its blunt unseeing head, and its awful voice reverberated in the narrow space.

Silence and Frost fired their disrupters. The vivid energy beams seared through the alien's vast body, exploding the black flesh and spattering it across the walls, and didn't even slow it down. Silence and Frost put away their guns, drew their swords and raised their force shields. They stood ready to meet the alien, knowing they couldn't hope to stand against it, but doing it anyway because it was their job and their duty, and because there wasn't anything else they could do, after all. The alien burst into the room, into what had been the heart of its web, its shell, and there was no time left for anything.

And then the Ashrai came.

Silence walked in the metallic forest, each gold and bronze and silver tree blazing like a star. The trees were singing, and though he was not a part of it, still the song trembled in his bones and in his soul, as though it was something he had known and left behind, long ago. Sean and Frost and Diana walked with him, all of them glowing like the trees. Frost looked younger, happier, at ease with herself, and for the first time since he'd met her, she wore no weapons. No sword or gun or grenades. She looked almost naked without them, but her eyes were clear and untroubled. Sean looked much as he used to, in the days when they could still be friends, with nothing to separate them. He smiled at Silence, and there was understanding if not forgiveness in the outlaw's eyes. And Diana shone more brilliantly than any of them.

The Ashrai walked in the forest, dead but not gone, huge and awesome, with their gargoyle faces and massive bodies, clawed hands and piercing eyes. They sang in harmony with the trees, and power burned brightly in them. The song and the power roared in human and Ashrai alike, building and building, vast and potent, blazing so brightly they knew they had to use it soon or it would burn them all out. The force that drove them focused and concentrated in one person, and Silence had enough of himself left to be faintly surprised that the focus was Diana, not Carrion. Diana Vertue, inhumanly treated but still human, more of an esper than the Empire had ever allowed her to be, unbroken and above all still somehow innocent, with purity of heart and thought and purpose. The power blazed in her, and without rage or hatred she turned it on the alien from outside. It was in the forest too, burning in strange hues, silent and malignant. It shrank back as the song of the trees washed over it, pure and piercing in Diana's voice, and in a moment that seemed to last for ever, the alien's light guttered and went out and was gone.

And with the alien gone, a host of new voices sounded in the metallic forest; the 127 men and women of Base Thirteen, free at last from the terrible thing that had been done to them. Their lights flickered and went out one by one, and there was no sadness in their leaving. It was what they had hoped and prayed for, for so long. Two familiar faces smiled briefly; Stasiak and Ripper, bound together on one last journey. They saluted briefly, and were gone. Diana looked out over the Base, and reached casually down to lower the force Screen and stop the nuclear countdown. The clock stopped ticking and the bomb disarmed itself, and as simply as that, it was all over.

And then the Ashrai withdrew a little, and looked at John Silence, Captain of the *Darkwind*, ambassador of the Empire. The man who gave the order for the scorching of Unseeli. Silence stood alone, offering no explanation or defence, because he had none. He didn't ask for mercy for himself because he expected none, but he did ask it for Frost and Diana, because both were innocent, in their way. They smiled and came to stand beside him, facing the Ashrai, because, after all, they belonged together. And that just left Carrion, once called Sean, standing alone between Ashrai and humanity, both and neither. The outlaw leaned on his staff and said nothing.

He passed judgement on us, said a multitude of voices. *Now it shall be passed on him. He must die.*

No, said Frost. *It was his duty.*

No, said Diana. *He has made atonement.*

He must die.

No, said Carrion. *He is my friend.*

As you wish.

And then the Ashrai were gone, and the lights in the trees seemed a little less magnificent without them. And Silence and Carrion and Frost and Diana turned and walked away from the metallic forest, knowing that the memory of its song would always be with them now, wherever they went and whatever they became.

CHAPTER ELEVEN

All the Ghosts Come Home to Roost

They left Base Thirteen, stepping one at a time past the unmoving metal doors, and stood blinking owlishly at the evening twilight. Dark clouds filled the sky, filtering the light into shades of grey, but even so it seemed uncomfortably bright after so long in the darkness of the Base. The sun was a crimson ball riding low on the sky, but the metal trees still blazed fiercely against the falling night. The mists were thickening, moving slowly among the trees like restless thoughts. Three moons drifted high on the evening sky, pale and listless like the memory of sunlight.

Silence stretched slowly, feeling an almost physical relief now that the mission was over, and he could finally relax and wind down. It hadn't ended in quite the way he'd thought it would, but then, that was Unseeli for you. Things seemed to have worked out well enough. All that remained now was to return to the *Darkwind*, and spend his time in Quarantine working out a written report his superiors could believe. He had a feeling that might take some time. He looked across at Carrion. The outlaw stood alone, a little way from the others, his face calm, his gaze fixed on the metallic forest. His cloak hung about him like the folded wings of a bird of prey, and Silence thought he could still sense some of the deadly power Carrion had unleashed in the Base. He wasn't the man Silence remembered, and he didn't know whether to feel sad or relieved. The old Carrion had been desperately unhappy. But the outlaw had found something in his exile with the Ashrai, and Silence thought it might just be peace.

Investigator Frost was calmly running through an inventory of the weapons she'd used up in her fight against the alien and its offshoots. She still had a surprising number left, though Silence was damned if he knew where she'd hidden them about her person. And Diana Vertue, his ship's esper, his daughter, was staring out at the glowing metal trees with wide, fascinated eyes. Silence stirred uneasily as he saw something in her face of the cool alienness in Carrion's gaze. He looked out at the trees, and a faint echo of the Ashrai song moved within him. He knew the song would always be with him now, murmuring quietly in the depths of the back brain, where all the important instinctive decisions are made. But already the strength of the vision was fading, slipping away from him even as he tried to hold on to it. Perhaps that was for the best, after all. He couldn't have retained the song in all its power, and still have remained human. He'd seen what it had done to Carrion. And to Diana. He moved over to stand beside her, and she nodded politely to him before looking back at the trees.

'How do you feel, Diana?'

'Strange. Tired. Different. I don't know, Captain. I've got a lot to think about. I just wish we could have saved some of the Base personnel.'

'They were already dead long before we got here,' said Silence. 'At least we were able to set them free. That's something. I'm not sure how much I believe of what I saw when the Ashrai sang. I can't believe the alien had captured all those souls in its machines . . . but I'm glad we did the right thing, anyway.'

Diana nodded slowly. 'What will happen to the trees now, Captain?'

'They should be safe enough. That strange crystal-based stardrive you and Carrion found in the crashed alien ship changes everything. According to Carrion, it's vastly superior to ours. We're going to have to study and duplicate the alien drive, if we're to stand any chance against the aliens. And since this new stardrive apparently doesn't need the heavy metals our drives use, we don't need Unseeli's trees any more. I suppose there'll still be some mining here, as long as some of us are still using the old drive, but that'll die out, over the years. Unseeli will finally be safe from the Empire, for the simplest of reasons;

because Unseeli has nothing the Empire wants any more.'

'There's going to be a war with the aliens, isn't there,' said Diana, and there was no question in her voice.

'It's inevitable,' said Silence. 'As their species spreads out, looking for new spawning grounds to colonise and dominate, they're bound to encounter human planets. And since their whole existence is dependent on taking over and transforming every other life form they come across, I don't really see any chance of our two species agreeing to coexist. You saw the alien's home planet, in that memory crystal. There's no place in their life cycle for peace or diplomacy or mutual interests. They live only to expand, transform and assimilate everything they encounter. They probably wouldn't even recognise us as a sentient species; just new genetic material to add to their melting pot. They're a deadly threat to the whole Empire, and the Empire has always known how to deal with threats. There's a war coming all right, and it's going to be the bloodiest, deadliest war in our species' history; a war for the survival of humanity.'

'Right,' said Carrion. 'At long last the Empire has found a species as deadly and single-minded as itself. The war will never end till one species or the other is extinct.'

'Right,' said Frost. 'It's going to be magnificent. I can hardly wait.'

There was a pause, as the others looked at each other and decided they were going to pretend she hadn't said that. Silence cleared his throat.

'I think we'd better get back to the pinnace. It'll be night soon, and this place is cold enough during the day. Odin; I take it you're still listening in. How are the repairs going? Are you ready for us to board yet?'

'The repair situation is well in hand, Captain. The pinnace is ready to take off at a moment's notice. However, I'm afraid I can't let any of you back on board.'

There was a long pause, significant with meaning, and when Silence finally spoke, his voice was calm and even and very controlled. 'What do you mean, you can't let us back on board? You agreed that if we saved the Base and its contents from destruction, you'd take us back to Quarantine on the *Darkwind*.'

'I lied,' said the AI. 'My programming allows me to be flexible under emergency conditions. It was important to motivate you to protect Base Thirteen and its contents, so I lied. I never had any intention of letting you back on board. I'm afraid all of you are contaminated by this new alien species, and I must protect the *Darkwind*.'

'Listen, computer,' said Silence. 'Conditions on Unseeli after nightfall are practically sub-polar, and the Base is a mess. You can't just abandon us here.'

'Yes I can, Captain. My programming is most explicit on this matter.'

'To hell with that,' said Frost. 'Computer; Code Red Seven. Acknowledge.'

'Code Red Seven acknowledged, Investigator.'

'Power up the pinnace and stand ready to transport us all back to the *Darkwind*, to start our Quarantine.'

'Yes, Investigator.'

Silence looked at Frost. 'Code Red *Seven*? Even I don't have that kind of Security clearance.'

'Neither do I,' said Frost. 'I stole it, some time back. I always thought it would come in handy. And anyway, Investigators are supposed to use their initiative. The computer will do what it's told now. Won't you, Odin?'

'Yes, Investigator. I will serve you to the limits of my programming. I will follow your orders . . .'

'Computer.'

'Yes, Investigator?'

'Shut up.'

'Yes, Investigator.'

Silence looked at Carrion, and indicated with his head that he wanted to talk to Carrion in private, a little away from the others. The outlaw nodded, and the two of them moved unhurriedly away from Frost and Diana.

'My offer of a Pardon still stands,' said Silence quietly. 'Your experience in defeating the alien makes you a valuable asset. The Empire is going to need

what you know. You could come back with us, Sean.
With me. Rejoin the Service, become an Investigator
again. Things have changed in the ten years you've
been away. You could write your own ticket, Sean.
And we could be together again, just like old times.
What do you say?'

The outlaw looked at him for a long moment. 'My
name is Carrion, Captain. Sean died a long time ago. I
have no wish to return to the Empire, with all its
petty politics, hatreds and destructive rages. I don't
belong there any more. I've walked the path of the
Ashrai for ten years now. I can't go back to being
human again. To being only human. Before you
came, I was a part of the song of the trees, of the
Ashrai. I'd forgotten most of my past. You're a ghost
to me, John; an echo of a past that no longer has any
real meaning for me. I haven't just left humanity; I've
moved beyond it.'

'Then where will you stand, during the war?' said
Silence.

'With my people,' said Carrion. 'With the Ashrai.'

'I've missed you, Sean. Please. I don't want to lose
you again.'

'You lost me ten years ago, John. It's too late to try
and find me now. Neither of us are the people we
used to be. I belong here now.'

'In other words,' said Frost, 'he's gone native.'

Silence and Carrion looked round sharply, both of

them startled. Neither of them had heard Frost
approach, but then she was an Investigator, after all.

'You're welcome to stay here, if you wish,' said
Carrion to the Investigator. 'The song is strong in you.
I could teach you the ways of the Ashrai, open your
mind to wonders you've never even dreamed of.
There are treasures of the soul here, just waiting for
you to discover them.'

'No thanks,' said Frost. 'Aliens are for killing. It's
time to go, Captain.'

'Yes,' said Silence. 'I think it is.'

Diana came over to see what they were talking
about and looked, in confusion, from one silent face
to another. 'Captain . . . before we go back to the
pinnace, can I ask you a question?'

'Of course, esper. What is it?'

'Why do you call the AI Odin?'

'Because he only has one eye,' said Silence. Carrion
was the only one who smiled. Diana and Frost just
looked at each other blankly.

'Don't they teach mythology in the Empire any
more?' said Carrion.

'Not much,' said Silence. 'A lot of it's been cen-
sored, or adjusted. Our superiors thought it might
give people ideas. Dangerous things, ideas.'

'Then perhaps it's time we made some new myths,'
said Carrion. 'We've started one here, today. A
hundred years from now, who we are and what we
did will be part of the history books. And how much

of us, the real us, will they remember? Or be allowed to remember. But truth lives on, through myths and legends, and our four ghosts will haunt the Empire long after we've gone.'

He nodded once to each of them, and strode off into the thickening mists, disappearing finally into the glowing metallic forest of Unseeli.

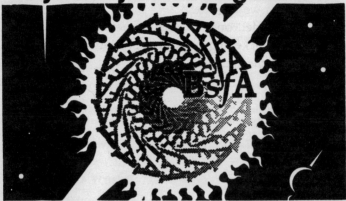